UNMASKED

BLAKE BRIER BOOK ONE

L.T. RYAN

with
GREGORY SCOTT

LIQUID MIND MEDIA, LLC

For information contact:

Contact@ltryan.com

https://LTRyan.com

https://www.facebook.com/JackNobleBooks

1

The 2-train pulled into the Wall Street station at 8:01 a.m. and the doors opened. Eli Butler forced his way through the Brooklyn-bound, squeezing himself out onto the platform. For six steps, he walked behind a woman looking down at her phone, apparently oblivious to the human traffic patterns she was disrupting.

He saw a gap and made his move. He passed the sluggish woman, then darted left and right around the other meanderers. He fell in behind a smartly dressed man, Wall Street type, who moved swiftly and blazed a path through the crowd. Eli drafted him, taking advantage of the space he carved out as they both maneuvered in a synchronized zigzag pattern.

Eli tried to will the sweat from beading up on his forehead. The perspiration was caused partly from the exertion and partly from what his boss would say when he was late for the third time this week.

The daily hour-long trip from 242nd Street on the 1-train stayed on schedule. The delay arose when transferring to the 2-train at Chambers Street.

Eli repeated flimsy excuses to himself as he climbed the stairs and emerged into the cacophony of the city street. Despite his tardiness, he paused for a moment and took a deep, meditative breath. Eli loved the smell of New York City in the morning. It was a mixture of car fumes, asphalt, exhaust from the various restaurants' kitchens and, strangely enough, urine. He was not sure if he imagined the urine smell, but he distinctly detected it, nonetheless.

The smell of the city street always calmed him, even as he stressfully hurried toward an inevitable ass-chewing. It never failed to give him pause. It made him consider that there is a bigger picture, a larger world to be experienced.

He jogged the last one hundred yards to the corner of Wall Street and Water Street. He breezed into the lobby of 95 Wall Street and called the elevator. The building seemed eerily empty at 8:09 a.m. A marked difference from the usual chaos of 7:55.

The elevator arrived and Eli rode it alone to the fourteenth floor. The doors opened to a brightly lit vestibule. Frosted glass obscured the busy operation bustling behind the semi-opaque inner doors. Lettering was etched in the large glass panels: "IPFG Financial – Corporate Security Headquarters."

Eli was truly appreciative to have his job and the hundreds of hours of training that came along with it. He knew, with only a high school diploma under his belt, it was better than many of his other options. Plus, as a video surveillance specialist, monitoring over three hundred IPFG branches and facilities, Eli had season tickets to what he routinely called *"the shit show,"* robberies, car crashes, domestic flights, and even the occasional workplace romantic encounter.

He was operating the video camera controls during an event one year prior in which an irate former IPFG employee, Tomas Shegrun, walked into a Tulsa satellite office with an AR-15. The guy's intention was to kill his former boss, VP of Sales, Steve Winters, but he never got the chance.

Serendipitously, Winters had called in sick that day. The word was that he was nursing a hangover. A couple of witnesses later reported seeing him doing an uncounted number of brightly-colored shots at a twenty-year high school reunion the night before.

In the end, Shegrun ended up firing a few rounds into Winters' desk and computer screen, but otherwise left the employees unharmed. After failing to locate his target, he fled the building only to be apprehended a few minutes later, due, in part, to information provided by Eli Butler.

Eli received an award from the company and was later invited to a banquet held at a Washington, D.C., hotel, but he could not afford to make the trip. He was secretly proud of the recognition, even though he disparaged the whole premise whenever it was mentioned by his coworkers.

For Eli, there was a sharp distinction between being appreciative and being satisfied. Eli wanted real action. To be physically involved, not looking on like some perverted voyeur. He had been trying for several years to land a job with the New York City Police Department but kept falling short for one reason or another.

On his latest try, he passed the written exam, the physical agility, and the polygraph, but was rejected after the psychological test. He was not sure exactly why he failed. They didn't tell him specifically. He did not feel crazy, *but then again*, he thought at the time, *you'd have to be relatively sane to be aware that you weren't.*

Despite the rejection, Eli wasn't deterred. He probably should have been, but it wasn't in his nature. He was fond of the cliché, *"If at first you don't succeed"* and he'd surely come to live by it.

Eli opened the big glass doors, turned right, and made a beeline past reception and the main floor of the office, toward the video surveillance department. He passed by Julie and Philippa, who didn't even turn in their cubicles to acknowledge him. He noticed his boss, Matthew Peterson, across the large room by the long windows overlooking a panoramic view of lower Manhattan. Eli was relieved that Peterson's attention seemed to be directed toward a group of four individuals huddled around him. Peterson was motioning toward the windows while speaking, as if he were explaining the layout of the city to the group.

Matthew Peterson was in his sixties and the only hair he had left was wrapped around his head near his ears, leaving the top of his head a gleaming, polished orb. Peterson stood about 5'10", a full five inches shorter than Eli's lanky frame. However, the head of security's broad shoulders and deep voice gave him a commanding presence. His temper was often short, and Eli preferred to avoid having it directed at him.

The sum of Eli's height, "high and tight" haircut, and permanent five o'clock shadow should have made him an imposing character himself, but when he spoke, he came across as a bit simple, giving him a disarming quality.

With Peterson distracted, Eli scurried down the short hallway and opened the heavy door marked, "VSCCC."

"It's about time," said Andre Lopes as he grabbed his bag and headed toward the door. "Oh, and Peterson's pissed."

Eli could tell Andre was irritated. Who wouldn't be? It was policy that no one could leave until relieved by the oncoming shift. Andre had clearly had enough. His eyes were sunken and glassy, a byproduct of staring at the wall of nearly fifty screens for hours on end. Eli knew the feeling. The burning, itching, dry eyes. The dull migraine headache, being staved off only by a steady diet of Excedrin and coffee.

Eight hours in the darkened room was bad enough during the day, but Eli couldn't fathom how Andre Lopes and the other third-shifters could stomach staring at motionless screens throughout the night.

Eli had covered a shift for Andre once and barely made it three hours before falling into a ridiculous cycle of dozing and startling himself awake. He'd bounce up with vigor and devote his full energy and attention to his assigned task. No more than thirty seconds would go by before he found himself powerless to stop his eyelids from drooping under their own weight again. Day or night, the fact that the entire interior of the room, aside from the dark gray commercial tile on the floor, had been painted black, made it feel like a gloomy, albeit spacious, tomb.

"Sorry Dre, I owe you," Eli called out as the door was closing behind his zombified friend.

Eli sat in the large, swiveling chair as he scooted himself up to the crescent-shaped desk. Three identical desks sat side-by-side in the middle of the room. There was at least fifteen feet of empty space on all sides, more on the side facing the video screens. For the most part, only one desk was used, although all three stations offered identical control capability. There was only one specialist manning the control center during each shift, and all of them preferred the center console. Eli felt it to be more symmetrical sitting in the middle. It gave him a more uniform view of the wall of screens in front of him.

Eli adjusted the angle of the four computer screens mounted to the desk, logged into the system and, remaining faithful to his daily ritual, began rearranging the various software windows into positions with which he was comfortable. Like every other morning, he lamented that the developers of the security control software, GeoNet, had not yet built in a way for separate users to save their user interface preferences. But in truth, he kind of enjoyed the ritual. And anything else that would zap a few extra minutes from the day.

Andre had already set the system to autorotation, which systematically looped through views of the various facilities, displaying the live video feeds on the gigantic wall of plastic, LEDs, and liquid crystal.

Feeling settled, Eli brought up the online edition of "Guns and Ammo," and scanned the recent questions and comments in the site's forum. Eli volunteered as a moderator for the online forum and would visit the site several dozen times a day. He had poured many hours and dollars into this hobby over the past few years. As a collector, Eli had amassed a decent inventory of pistols, revolvers, and rifles, a luxury that was afforded to him by virtue of being single.

He typed out a quick response, correcting a poster's misstatement that the velocity of the 5.56 NATO round was 2800 ft/s. "I believe the velocity of the 5.56 is 3,025 ft/s. You might be thinking of the 7.62," he wrote.

Eli sent the reply, closed the web browser, and got up from the desk. He walked over to the back of the room and loaded a coffee pod into the Keurig machine set up on a small folding table.

The door opened with an accompaniment of laughing voices and streaming light.

"And this is the crown jewel of our department. Our state-of-the-art Video Surveillance Command and Control Center," Peterson said to the group. "Around here we call it the cockpit."

One member of the group let out a slight chuckle before sheepishly trailing off, realizing Peterson was not making a joke.

Startled by the loud entry, Eli's leg muscles twitched as if he were going to sprint and leap into his chair. Instead, he stood by the coffee machine and lifted his hand in a meek wave.

"This is Mr. Butler. He is one of our specialists," Peterson continued. "Butler, bring up number two three two."

Eli rushed to his station and punched at the keyboard. The wall of screens flickered to display every angle covered by the forty-eight cameras installed in the downtown Los Angeles branch.

"This room was custom built to span two floors, in order to have the ceiling clearance to fit these forty-eight screens," Peterson ran through his usual spiel. "Specifically, to accommodate our largest coverage areas. Two facilities have forty-eight camera angles: Los Angeles, California and St. Petersburg, Russia. More than any other building in our purview. But that's not the impressive part. Each camera records a three-hundred-and-sixty-degree view in 5K resolution, allowing us to pan and zoom into almost every inch of our three hundred forty-two branches and facilities."

"That's pretty impressive," one of the group said, while jotting down something in a leather padfolio.

"Let me give you a demonstration. Do you see that man there, with the gray jacket and yellow tie, walking toward the staircase?" Peterson asked as the group nodded. "Butler, follow him."

Eli's command of the system was uncanny. He could move between cameras and intuitively coerce the massive network to do his bidding. He grabbed a small box off the desk, which consisted of a joystick and a keypad with a dozen backlit buttons. One of the four screens in front of him flashed to a video feed and displayed an over-head view of the subject climbing a marble staircase, the word "Output" superimposed over the image.

Eli's eyes darted from the wall of video to the desktop monitor and back but never glanced at the device in his hands. He punched at the various keys with his left hand as his right manipulated the joystick controller.

The group murmured as Eli switched views, panned, and tracked the unknowing subject. He followed the man into an office and trained another camera on him as he sat down at a mahogany desk. Eli zoomed in tight as the man picked up a telephone receiver. Eli then abruptly panned the camera toward the wall and left it there.

"Who did he call?" Peterson asked.

The group didn't respond. After a brief pause for effect, Peterson motioned to Eli.

Eli clicked the keys in a quick burst and the video ran back to the point at which the subject was approaching the desk. The video stopped and then ran forward, replaying the sequence of actions the group had just witnessed. The subject picked up the phone but, instead of the camera panning toward the blank wall, Eli pressed and turned the joystick, zooming in until the keypad of the phone filled the screen.

The man tapped the ten digits into the phone's keypad. Eli placed the controller onto the desktop, grabbed the mouse and clicked a couple of on-screen buttons. The close-up view of the phone's keypad and the man's dialing finger played in a loop in slow motion. Peterson called out each number with a dramatic intonation.

Eli sat back in his chair and turned to look at the group. The corners of his mouth turned up in a subtle proud smile. Peterson also let a slight grin show, obviously pleased with the improvised skit he and his employee had just performed.

"Any questions?" Peterson asked. Without waiting for a response, he continued, "Okay, then. Let's move upstairs to the computer forensics department. I think you'll find it quite interesting."

The group began filing out of the door. Peterson turned back toward Eli, his smile instantly leaving his face.

"Your shift starts at 8:00 a.m. Butler. You and I will speak later," he said in a hushed voice.

Uneasy, Eli turned his attention back to the video panels. Instead of re-engaging the autorotation, he punched in the numbers for several of the more active facilities. Miami, Chicago, Dallas. Business as usual. Satisfied that all was well in the world, he let the computer take over the rotation.

He opened the Google Chrome browser and dragged the cursor toward the favorites bar link labeled "Guns and Ammo." Before he clicked, the loud screech of a hold-up alarm echoed through the cavernous room. White lights, mounted in the corners of the room, began flashing and the forty-eight monitors switched to display the thirty-five cameras covering the interior and exterior of 2100 L St. NW, Washington, D.C.

The busy D.C. branch had not been one of the usual false-alarm offenders, but Eli was very familiar with the location. In addition to the public bank branch being located on the ground floor, the building housed one of the corporation's largest data centers.

Eli glanced at each of the panels, observing people move about the nondescript offices, board rooms, elevators, and hallways. The incessant screeching continued to uncomfortably rattle his eardrums.

Then he saw it.

Eli snatched the controller from the desk and, with a couple of keystrokes, plucked one of the main lobby camera views off the wall and deposited it onto his desktop monitor.

He zoomed in and sat, for a moment, staring motionless with mouth agape. This was going to be a bad day.

2

E li, his eyes pinned open in disbelief, reached for his headset and put it on, never glancing away from the scene unfolding on the screen in front of him. He clicked the mouse to dismiss the alarm, slid his hand across the desk until he felt the desktop telephone, and pulled it closer to him.

He began to dial 911 but hung up before the call went through, realizing the call would only connect him to the local NYPD dispatch center. He brought up a browser window and typed "Washington D.C. police" into the browser bar. Google listed "Metropolitan Police Department of the District of Columbia" at the top of the screen.

He dialed the emergency number by feel as he turned his attention back to the live video feed.

"D.C. Metro, Call-taker Ward, how can I assist you?" a woman answered.

"Hi. Yes. This is Eli Butler with IPFG Financial Security. I need to report a robbery in progress. 2100 L Street Northwest."

"Yes sir," Ward responded curtly. "We've received the alarm and have officers en route."

"Okay. Good. I'm looking at a live video feed, I can give you some more information if you need it," Eli said, not sure if he was overstepping his bounds.

The line went quiet for a moment. Eli could hear muffled conversation in the background.

"Yes sir. Stay on the line and tell me what's going on. I'll relay any information to the dispatcher. Is everyone all right there?" she said.

"I'm not there. I'm in New York City. But yes, it looks like it, for the moment. Like I said, I'm looking at live video from inside."

"Okay. What do you see, sir?"

Peterson burst through the door. He flew into the room and stopped a few feet from Eli.

"What's happening?" Peterson said loudly while looking over the wall of video screens. He turned to Eli for his response.

Eli pointed at his headset mic and mouthed the words "D.C. Metro."

Peterson, abandoning his question, moved to the desk to the left of Eli and picked up the phone. He dialed a number and Eli heard him say frantically, "get me Alders."

Eli zoomed the camera out to get a wide-angle view of the entire lobby. He spoke to the call-taker on the other end of the line. "There's five guys. I think they're guys. They're wearing masks and gloves. And dark hoodie sweatshirts with the hoods up over their heads. They're all armed."

"You're sure they're armed?" Ward questioned.

"Yes. Absolutely armed. With assault rifles. If I had to guess, I'd say H&K 416s, but I guess they could be modified M4s or something else entirely. From this angle I can see that at least two of them are carrying a sidearm." Eli zoomed in on the holster attached to one of the gunmen's belts. "Maybe Glocks or Smith M&Ps. Hard to say."

Eli could hear the woman calling out to someone else in the room. "Have 'em stage. This guy says there's five inside, heavily armed."

"What are they doing now?" Ward asked back into the phone.

"They're moving around the lobby. It looks like they're forcing the customers to lie on the ground." Eli could see one of the gunmen raise his rifle into the air. Several muzzle flashes were visible on the high-resolution feed. "Oh no, they're blowing off rounds."

"Sir, is someone shot?" Her tone became increasingly more charged.

"No, no, they're firing into the ceiling," he said.

Eli heard a more muffled conversation.

"Sir, can you describe the suspects?"

"I told you. They're all identical. Wearing masks, black- or dark-colored hoodies and blue jeans. Two of them have black backpacks."

"What kind of masks?" Ward probed. "Ski masks?"

"No. They're plastic, I think. All white, except for some green blood or something coming from the eyes. I'm taking some screen-shots. If you want, I can email them."

"Sir, officers are arriving now. Where in the building are they?" she asked, ignoring the suggestion.

"They're in the main lobby. That's where the public bank branch is located. The rest of the building is just offices and computer equipment. Server rooms and that kind of thing."

Eli noticed that two of the men, the ones with the backpacks, had broken off from the others. One moved toward the front doors and the other headed to the rear exit. Eli manipulated his mouse and, after a few clicks, had rearranged two of the screens on the wall so the views of the front and rear doors were physically adjacent.

Eli watched as both men rooted around in their backpacks and pulled out gray rectangular blocks. The men attached the blocks to the wall just inside their respective entryways. They inserted a silver cylinder into each block and unspooled a red rope. Eli thought it looked like the rope lights he had bought at Home Depot to run along the railing on his patio. He knew he was no expert in explosives, but he thought it would be pretty obvious to anyone what the two men were planning.

"Tell the cops not to go in through the doors. I think they've set up explosives inside the doors," Eli warned.

Eli heard Ward relaying the information.

The three other men moved toward the teller counter, stepping over patrons who were lying on the floor, face down with hands interlaced at the back of their heads. Eli could see three tellers lying on the floor behind the counter. He glanced at the number of exterior feeds and could see several police cruisers gathering outside the building. Some of the officers had taken positions behind their vehicles and were pointing long guns toward the building.

"They're at the teller counter saying something to the tellers. Looks like they're having them stand up."

Eli watched as the three women behind the counter stood up and approached their tills with their hands extended into the air. All three were around the same age, late twenties, early thirties. Each gunman had his rifle trained on a different teller.

"I think they're having them get the money from the drawers," Eli updated.

All six stood completely still. Three tellers with hands raised. Three riflemen holding their weapons to their faces in a standoff tableau.

Then, without warning and with the precision of a firing squad, Eli saw a flash from all three muzzles simultaneously. The beige wall behind the teller area instantly turned a sickening shade of red. Small red spots appeared in the centers of the three women's light-colored blouses and rapidly grew until almost completely saturating the thin fabric of each garment. Eli could see the look of pain and disbelief on their faces. Haunting expressions that emoted an indescribable sadness.

The three women clutched at their chests and, one after another, slumped over or fell to the ground. Motionless.

"No! No! No!" Eli cried. "Why?"

"What happened, sir?" Ward asked with reciprocal urgency.

Eli looked to his left to see Peterson staring at the video wall. His right hand lay in his lap, still squeezing the handset of the phone. Eli felt as if the horror of what they just witnessed had entered his body through his eyes and wrapped around his soul like a boa constrictor. Peterson's eyes welled up, and Eli covered most of his face with both hands.

"They didn't take the money," Eli said quietly, half to himself and half to Peterson. "They didn't take the money," he repeated more loudly into the headset microphone.

"You've got to get in there," Eli said, the pace and pitch of his voice rising back to peak levels. "They shot 'em. They killed 'em for no reason."

"Who? Who's shot?" Ward interrupted.

"The tellers. All at once. They executed them. They just freakin' executed them." Eli could feel himself shaking. It was as if the innocent women weren't actually dead until he said the words, solidifying the reality.

"They're moving. I think they're going upstairs," he said, as he watched the three shooters begin to move past the elevators, toward the access door for the stairwell. "You've got to get in there, now!"

"Is there another entrance," Ward asked, her voice remaining calm and collected.

"No. Not at ground level. There is an access door to the stairwell on the roof, if someone could get up there."

For a moment, Eli thought of the ridiculousness of the proposition, but then considered that the Washington, D.C., police department probably had a helicopter. The roof might be a viable option. "Do you have a helicopter?"

"Well, yes. But sir, I'm only relaying the information. How the officers approach this is up to the commanders on the ground. Can you still see them?"

Eli abandoned his computer, stood up, and walked around the desk. He leaned back against the sturdy piece of furniture and stared up at the towering wall of light.

"Okay, I'll just describe everything that's happening. You do with it what you can. Right now, the two guys with the backpacks are still in the lobby. The other three are climbing the stairs."

There was no interruption from the other end of the line.

"One of the backpack guys is crouching down over one of the people lying on the floor of the lobby, an older guy with gray hair and blue shirt. The guy's standing up. The old guy, I mean. The backpack guy is leading him toward the front."

Eli hoped he wasn't about to witness another senseless slaughter. He glanced at the stairwell monitors.

"The three guys in the stairwell are moving on to the third floor. That floor is part of the data center. There's nothing on three but some climate-controlled computer rooms."

An employee sat at a desk just outside the secure data center area. The young man appeared to be typing away at a keyboard, unaware of the holdup alarm that had been triggered in the branch below.

"Do we have a phone number for that guy?" Eli pointed at the screen as he turned back to Peterson, who was still busy updating his bosses by telephone.

Eli saw the three gunmen traveling down the hallway, toward the oblivious young man. With the three of them lined up side-by-side, Eli could see that one of the three men was significantly taller than the other two.

"They're moving toward the data center. When they turn the next corner, they're going to run right into an employee who doesn't look like he knows they're coming," Eli said to Ward. "They're turning the corner. They shot him. They shot him in the face. He's still moving. No, never mind. One of the other two shot him again, four or five times. Point blank. Christ, these guys are complete savages."

He was amazed at the callousness and the complete lack of hesitation displayed by the masked men. The largest of the three had barely rounded the corner before he raised his rifle and casually murdered the young employee.

Eli could hear commotion on the other end of the line but did not get a verbal response from the call-taker. He felt himself becoming more effective at pushing the gruesomeness of what he was seeing out of his mind and focusing on his task of objective narration.

"They're taking something out of the dead guy's pocket. It's a keycard. They're using it to open the door to the server room."

He switched his attention to the monitors showing the inside of the secure area. There were multiple cameras covering the corridors between rows of large computer cabinets. Through the glass doors of the cabinets, blue, yellow, and green LED lights blinked and flickered. Eli continued to track the three men.

"One of the two shorter guys stayed in the hallway. The other is staying by the door, just inside the server room. The taller guy just pulled out a drawer with a keyboard from one of the racks. He's typing on it."

Eli realized the masked men weren't looking for money.

"This place probably holds a ton of customer information. Bank accounts, credit cards. They're trying to steal it all, I bet," Eli said, inserting his own theories into the situation.

"Okay, listen," Ward said, finally re-entering the conversation. "The helicopter is being deployed. It's about ten minutes out. We're going to need your help. When the time comes, we're going to patch you in to the SWAT commander directly. While he and his team are making entry from the roof, you'll be the eyes. Okay?" Ward asked rhetorically.

"Yes. Of course," Eli said.

"Keep doing what you're doing," Peterson interjected in a hushed voice as he stood up from the desk. "I'll be back. Corporate's filled in. The jet is on its way. We're setting up a war room in the conference room next door, but be prepared. This room may be getting real crowded, real quick," he said as he hurried out the door.

Eli looked over the screens and noticed that while he was watching the server room, the two masked men in the lobby had lined up all eight hostages, in two lines of four, in front of the two front doors. Eli noticed that the gunmen themselves had not crossed in front of the glass doors, even when planting the explosives. He assumed they were aware that snipers would have already been in position, waiting for an opportunity to take them out.

"The hostages are lined up by the front doors. The officers should be able to see them through the glass."

Eli worried that the gunmen were staging a show. Getting ready to execute the eight hostages in full view of the police and, God forbid, the news media. He realized why Peterson had been frantically conferring with corporate management. Something Peterson had said on the phone had finally registered in his brain. "PR nightmare," was the phrase he used. Eli had no doubt there would be backlash.

"The guys on the third floor are still in the same spots," he continued with his update. "Are you still there?"

"Still here. Go ahead," Ward responded.

"The two in the lobby are standing against the wall on either side of the front doors. The hostages are all still standing there. Wait, they're moving toward the door. They're walking out the front doors! The guys in the masks aren't moving, they're just letting all of them leave." The tone of Eli's voice relayed his disbelief.

Through the external cameras, Eli could see the hostages emerging through the doors. As each hit the open air, they began sprinting away from the building. Several officers came out from their cover and pulled the fleeing people away and toward a large coach bus painted with the words "Metropolitan Police Mobile Command Center." Several officers intercepted them as they boarded the bus, cloaking them in large red blankets.

"They're all out," Eli said to Ward triumphantly.

"Is there anyone left in the building?" Ward asked.

Eli scanned the screens and quickly counted out a rough figure.

"There are about thirty employees in the building on different floors. But no one's left on the first and third." Eli paused at the gravity of why no one was left in those areas.

"The guys in the lobby still haven't moved. I mean, at all. The three upstairs are moving down the hallway toward the stairwell."

"The helicopter is in the air and is two minutes out. We're working on getting the patch in place now."

"Okay, got it. They're in the stairwell. Going back down. They passed by floor two, that's good news at least." He paused. "And they're coming back into the lobby."

Eli watched as the two masked men by the front doors moved toward the center of the bank floor. They flanked the other three men. Eli felt like he was watching a silent movie of a military color guard without the flags. The five men pushed back the hoods from their heads, exposing bald, pasty white scalps.

"What the hell are they doing?" Eli said out loud. "They dropped their rifles on the ground and are standing at attention. They're looking right at me."

"Looking at you?" Ward said.

"Looking right at the camera. This is creepy. Those weird masks don't help," Eli replied.

Eli really did feel uneasy. Even though he knew it was impossible, he felt like they could see him watching them. In any case, it was obvious that they knew someone was.

"Okay. Sir, I'm disconnecting, you're being patched in with Sgt. Delgrasso. Thank you," Ward said with a sigh of relief that her responsibility was being released.

Eli stared into the screen. Glared into the white, plastic faces, green tears streaming down the cheeks, and wondered what kind of monsters hid behind them. Then he witnessed something he never saw coming. Never would have been able to concoct in his wildest imagination.

In one fluid, almost imperceptible movement, all five men simultaneously drew their pistols from the holsters, jammed them under their chins, and pulled the triggers. The tops of their bald heads exploded, sending a red mist of blood and brain matter into the air. The mist lingered as the five limp bodies fell to the floor.

"No need, Miss Ward," Eli said solemnly. "It's over.

3

A constant flood of sweat crested Blake Brier's brow and flowed unimpeded into his eyes. Blake focused on the stinging feeling and fought the urge to blink. He was accustomed to extreme, unblinking focus under the crushing stress of life and death. As quickly as the grit surged inside of him, it receded into the nostalgia from which it came.

He exhaled fully, as if performing a meditation ritual. As his lungs expanded, he smirked at himself for the almost contrived sense of contentment he felt. A contentment he always felt while lying under a two hundred eighty-pound barbell. The sweat in Blake Brier's eyes on this day was of his own making, his own daily test. No lives hung in the balance. Those days were a million miles behind him.

Blake replaced the bar on its perch after his final rep. He laid still for several moments as his mind wandered. *What the hell is the purpose of eyebrows?* Blake devoted another half a second of his attention to the notion before he became conscious of the fact that his mind had wandered.

For many years, his mind had worked in a peculiar way. He had the ability to focus on complex problems for hours on end but, absent such stimulation, was struck by what he often referred to as "a touch of the ol' ADD." Of course, he had never been diagnosed. This may or may not have had something to do with the fact that he hadn't been to a doctor's office in years.

Blake hopped off the bench, toweled off, and headed for the juice bar. He would shower at home. It was only a five-minute drive and he wasn't particularly fond of the locker room crowd, a bunch of sixty- to seventy-year-old men who never seemed to actually migrate out to the gym floor. They'd unpack what seemed like four years' worth of toiletry products and commence with their work, which, as far as Blake could tell, consisted of standing around buck-naked and staring at themselves in the mirror.

Blake got in line behind a small twenty-something woman wearing a matching pink and black spandex outfit. The woman turned to glance at him, flashing a quick smile before returning to dictating her order of a soy-banana-flax-kale power shake. The woman was in pretty good shape, but Blake calculated that, at her age, she probably didn't have to put a whole lot of work into it. At forty-three years old, he was no longer the beneficiary of such perks of youth.

The woman paid for her shake and hustled by. She flashed one more quick smile his way. He sauntered up to the counter with a swagger fueled by the woman's second glance.

Still got it.

He often got that type of reaction from women, but he knew it probably had less to do with some animal magnetism and more to do with his calm and confident boyish aura. He was often told he had a "friendly face." His six-foot-three, two-hundred-thirty-pound frame might have seemed imposing in other settings, but not in this room. The juice heads crowding the dumbbell racks against the back wall of the gym dwarfed him. What did stand out, Blake figured, was not just his bright red hair, but also the bright red beard he had been growing for the past four months.

If anything, that's worthy of a double take.

Blake ordered a protein shake and swiped his debit card through the card-reader. The machine spit back the harsh response. "Declined." *Don't tell me, another fraud alert.* He replaced the card in his wallet and produced a credit card.

Swipe. "Declined."

Blake was not easily rattled, and this moment would certainly not be an exception, but he did feel the slightest warmth flush through his skin in spite of himself. He was well acquainted with the types of technical errors that crop up in payment networks, but he didn't particularly like the idea of appearing to anyone as some kind of deadbeat. A "crumb bum" as his father used to say.

The cashier shot him a dirty look, but what he didn't know was that Blake typically kept around two hundred thousand dollars in his bank account. Old habits.

You never know when you're going to need a ton of cash, and quick.

But the fact remained that Blake only carried two cards, and both had rudely rejected him. The cashier tightly gripped the freshly prepared protein shake as if he was afraid that Blake was going to try to grab it and run.

"I'll cover him," a soft, sweet voice came from over Blake's shoulder.

The sound of her voice slipped into his ears and rattled around in his gut. He knew that voice. He knew it well.

"Jo," he said, before turning around to confirm his prediction.

It had been ten years since he'd laid eyes on Anja Kohler, but he couldn't find a single difference in her appearance. If Blake didn't know Anja was thirty-eight years old, he'd swear she was the same twenty-eight-year-old girl he had once shared his bed with. Her blonde hair and sharp German features were every bit as striking as the day he first met her.

"How've you been, Blake?"

"Great, really great. Wow, you look great." *Ugh. Too many greats.*

"Yeah, uh, you too."

Blake's mind wandered back to the day that Anja Kohler broke off their five-year relationship and stepped into the taxicab she summoned to take her to the Washington, D.C., townhouse they once shared.

At some point, he had made a mental list of the things he regretted in his life. Although he was grateful it was a short list, he tended to remind himself of it frequently. There were no more than three things on his list. Watching the girl he called "Jo" drive out of his life was one of them.

Anja picked up a protein bar and paid for it, along with Blake's shake. She handed it to him.

"Thank you, Jo. I've gotta figure out what the hell's going on with my cards. So, what are you doin' here? Are you back?"

"Well, yeah, I guess I'm back." Anja glanced at her watch. "But I've gotta run, got called in. We'll catch up, just call me."

Anja scribbled a telephone number on the back of her business card. Blake took the card and, once again, watched her leave.

He looked at the front of the card. It read "Anja Kohler, Special Agent, Federal Bureau of Investigation."

She's still at it.

Blake leaned against the wall next to a trash can while he quickly sucked down his shake. He tossed the plastic cup into the trash and had turned to leave when he noticed that no one in the gym seemed to be moving. They were all standing with their necks craned toward the nearest flat-panel screen mounted above a treadmill or stairclimber.

He walked over to a screen which, a few moments before, was showing an old episode of "Judge Joe Brown," but had since been preempted by talking heads and scrolling news banners. He zoned in and absorbed the details, or pure speculation, being dramatically delivered by correspondents who rushed to the scene to catch whatever percentage of TV ratings were still up for grabs.

IPFG. Interesting.

4

Anja hadn't seen the video but was filled in on the phone during her ride in from Virginia.

She stood in the doorway of the IPFG Financial branch and marveled over the sheer size of the area that had been contaminated due to the suspects' dramatic finale.

The visual input of surveying the scene in person amalgamated with what she had seen in her mind's eye during the phone briefing.

Several FBI techs were already swarming, taking photographs and jotting notes into pocket-sized notebooks.

Before entering the building, Anja had donned a pair of rubber gloves and a pair of paper booties to both protect her shoes and limit contamination of the area.

Moving around inside without disturbing the scene, Anja thought immediately upon entering, *is going to be a trick.* The ceremonial salvo splattered blood and tissue within a thirty-foot radius, covering runner carpets, plush chairs for waiting customers, neatly organized paperwork on two glass countertops, intended for filling out deposit and withdrawal slips, and just about everything else in her line of sight. Then there was the tellers' area. Anja empathized with the crime scene techs who were tasked with processing, measuring, and documenting every inch of the chaotic scene.

"Hey, partner, glad you could make it," Andrew Harrison called out as he emerged from a door near the elevators.

Harrison wasn't exactly Anja's partner. The three-agent bank robbery unit based out of the D.C. field office was organized so that each agent managed their own caseload, independent of the other two. Each of them would draw on the others for assistance when needed. However, Anja found herself turning to Harrison more often than her other colleague, Jim Lawson. She found Harrison, as tactless as he could be at times, to be more competent than Lawson, who surprisingly had the most seniority and experience of the three of them.

Anja eased toward Harrison, trying to avoid disturbing anything.

"Hey buddy," Anja said warmly. "Is Lawson here yet?"

"No. He's not coming. Still at training in Alabama."

"Ah. So, it's just us. Where are we so far?" Anja asked.

"Well, it's not just us. Wells is upstairs. But I can fill you in a bit on what we've found out so far," Harrison replied.

Anja pursed her lips. "I was hoping to get a few minutes to sort this thing out before Wells showed up."

Oliver Wells was the Special Agent in Charge of the D.C. field office. Anja had a decent working relationship with him, enough so that he had approved her re-assignment there, but he tended to be high-strung, and Anja always felt this was added pressure that made it difficult to think critically and methodically, especially in the early stages of an investigation.

"This is some weird stuff," Harrison began. "It took an hour and a half to evacuate the building because the bomb techs had to clear explosives from the entryways first. They thought it was C4 but it turned out to be freakin' modeling clay."

Harrison let out a quick, hardy laugh.

Anja smirked, less at the idea of the clever ruse and more at Harrison's amusement over it.

"These five," pointing to the center of the room where the five deceased suspects laid in a grotesque heap, "kill every employee they come across, but let all of the customers go. What the hell is that?" he asked rhetorically. "They don't even ask or make any attempt to grab the money in the tills or the safe. Instead they go and mess around with a computer upstairs and then, of course, they all off themselves. And all of this in full view of the cameras. Makes perfect sense to me," Harrison said with a shrug and a smile to match the facetious remark.

"Okay. So, obviously, their whole goal was to get access to the computer room, but why kill the tellers?" Anja was puzzled.

"Well, this gets weirder. Much weirder. Once everyone was out, I debriefed a few of the employees who work in the IT department on the fourth floor. Most of them were useless. They had no idea what was going on down here. Anyway, I was talking to one of these geeky guys," Harrison flipped through his notebook, "Steven Reid. Computer engineer. This guy said he got a look at our dead friends here when he was being evacuated by SWAT and recognized the masks these guys were wearing. Said he's positive the masks are a kind of calling card used by a group called the CEA, Cryptocurrency Evangelist Army."

Harrison waited for a reaction, like he had just revealed the twist at the end of an M. Night Shyamalan movie. Anja's face remained expressionless.

"I'm not familiar," Anja said. "Well, neither was I. But I didn't want to let that dweeb know. So, I looked it up." Harrison referred back to his notepad. "The CEA, more commonly known as 'The Evangelists,' are a hacktivist group who support digital currency like Bitcoin. Basically, they pull stunts to draw attention to their cause. The goal being to replace traditional banking with this decentralized banking concept."

"Well, that could explain killing the bank employees and then releasing the customers. Some statements, like they're liberating the people from big finance, or something. Were the three tellers the only employees in the branch?" Anja asked.

"Yes. Well, no, actually. The manager was in his office over there. He locked himself in the closet. Lucky for him, no one went looking. We didn't even know he was in there until SWAT did the secondary search. There was also a loan officer who would normally be at the desk over there, but she ran next door for a bagel. By the time she came back, uniformed guys were already out front and stopped her from walking back in."

"So, do we know what they accessed?" Anja pressed.

"No. This guy Reid said if he got to a computer, he could give us an idea of what these guys were up to. But the building was already locked down."

"Can you point him out to me?" Anja asked.

"Yeah, come with me," Harrison said as he walked toward the rear exit door.

Anja followed Harrison out into the parking lot. The Red Cross had already arrived and set up several tents. Family members of employees were arriving to join their loved ones, who were being held on-site until they could be thoroughly debriefed.

"What nonsense," Harrison said, disapprovingly. "Counselors. Medics. Most of these people didn't even know anything was wrong until our guys made them leave the building."

"Well, aren't you just a bleeding heart?" Anja teased.

"There. That's Reid right there," Harrison interrupted, ignoring Anja's jab. He pointed out a slight man wearing a white shirt and yellow tie.

By his face, Anja guessed he was in his early thirties, but his full head of salt-and-pepper hair made her second guess her estimate. She approached.

"Hello, Mr. Reid. I'm Agent Kohler with the FBI. May I ask you a couple of questions?"

"Sure. No problem," Reid said.

"My partner tells me you recognized the masks the suspects were wearing."

"Of course. Everyone knows the Evangelists. Don't you have YouTube?"

"Yes," Anja said, awkwardly answering Reid's rhetorical question. She left it at that.

"Last year they launched a DDOS attack on us and about thirty other banks," Reid said. "At least, we believe it was them."

"Sorry," Anja interrupted, "DDOS?"

"It stands for Distributed Denial of Service," Reid explained. "Basically, an attacker uses a bunch of computers to flood the resources of the target system. Once the available bandwidth and resources are overwhelmed with the malicious traffic, the system can no longer respond to legitimate requests. Essentially, it takes the whole service off-line. This is particularly problematic, to say the least."

"Why is that?" Anja wasn't necessarily interested in the technical details, but she had learned long ago that the longer she could keep a person talking, the more useful the information became.

"Everyone knows IPFG is one of the largest online banking providers in the world, but what most people don't realize is we are also contracted by dozens of others to provide their online banking infrastructure. When you navigate to your bank's online portal, it may be branded as 'Such and Such Bank', but in reality, it's our developers, engineers, and infrastructure behind it. We have dozens of state-of-the-art data centers, located throughout the world, and we service literally tens of millions of customers. When the Evangelists attacked us last year, we were hosting all but one of the banks they went after," Reid explained.

"Do they have some kind of vendetta against your company?" Anja asked.

"Against the whole financial machine. Wall Street. Investment Banks. All of it. They post all this stuff about how banks are greedy and cryptocurrency will free people from tyranny."

"So, this so-called 'army' is a bunch of terrorists who kill innocent people to prove a point," Harrison chimed in.

"I don't exactly follow them," Reid clarified, "but I've never heard of the Evangelists being violent. Usually, they disrupt computer systems or maybe stage demonstrations. Like when they spray-painted that bull statue on Wall Street. Painted the entire thing green."

"Looks like they've graduated from vandalism to mass murder and stealing God knows how many people's financial information," Anja said.

"Well, if that's what they were after, they came to the wrong place," Reid said, matter-of-factly.

"What do you mean?" Anja probed.

"I mean, if you wanted to steal the millions of financial identities we manage, you wouldn't want to come here. Even though we do physically house a lot of data here, it's mostly infrastructure stuff. This building is our main development office. Engineers, developers, front-end staff, back-end staff, database people, testing. But the actual customer data isn't stored here. It's encrypted and stored in various other highly secure facilities around the world. The network is segmented in such a way that you can't even access that stuff from here. We mostly work with mock-up data. We're innovating software solutions, building artificial intelligence, you know, all the fun stuff. My point is, the most they were going to be able to do is set us back a bit. Everything is backed up hourly off-site."

Anja pulled out a notebook from her blazer pocket and jotted down a few ideas she intended to follow up on later.

"If you ask me," Reid continued, "my guess is they weren't trying to take anything. They were here to *add* something. Our network security is top-notch. Nobody is getting access to our systems from the outside. If you wanted to infect our systems with a virus, the only way that makes sense would be to introduce it to the network from the inside.

Anja looked at Harrison and realized that his eyes had glazed over at Reid's long-winded ramble. Probably within the first three seconds after Reid started talking. Anja sensed that Reid, his nerd-bravado notwithstanding, could probably provide some much-needed clarification.

"Mr. Reid, if I can get you back upstairs, can you determine what the subjects were trying to access?" Anja asked.

"Anja," Harrison interjected softly. He gave a gentle squeeze to her upper arm. "Is this a good idea?"

"These guys came here for something," Anja said. "Everything was meticulously planned. The fake explosives, the simultaneous suicides. I don't believe for one second that they just hadn't realized there was nothing here to steal."

Anja didn't wait for Harrison's approval. "Mr. Reid, please come with me," she said, walking toward the building.

Anja led Reid through the rear door of the branch. Harrison followed a few feet behind. Anja pressed the button to call the elevator.

Waiting for the elevator to churn its way down to the ground level, Anja tapped her fingers on her thigh with one hand while she rubbed her temples with the thumb and middle finger of the other, a typical tell that her brain was working in overdrive.

As the elevator opened, Reid began to move inside. Anja put out her arm, momentarily stopping him. She looked at Reid with determination. "Mr. Reid," she said, "you and I are going to find out what this was really about."

The three entered the elevator and Anja pressed the round, back-lit button labeled "4."

The doors closed, sealing out the commotion of the forensic investigation that ramped up into full swing.

5

B lake punched a code into the lock's keypad. The servo motor slid the bolt open with a sound that was reminiscent of a small robotic arm. The Bluetooth device communicated with the base station to disengage Blake's home alarm. He entered, relocked the door behind him, and reset the alarm for "Home" mode, activating the door and window sensors while disabling the motion detectors.

Even though he was sure he already locked the car, Blake depressed the lock button on his key fob and listened for the short blast of the Dodge Challenger's horn. He kicked off his sneakers, dropped his gym bag, and tossed his keys on a small table just inside the foyer of his three-story townhouse.

He walked past the stairway to the kitchen, checked that the back door was secure, and peaked through the blinds into the garden, not expecting to see anything out of the ordinary. Blake did a casual check of the rooms and determined that nothing was out of place. The procedure was half-hearted, nowhere near thorough, and would be utterly pointless if someone had been lying in wait for him.

He went through the motions not because he thought he was in danger, but because carrying out the pretense helped him relax. Over time, old habits — once necessary habits - solidified into superstitions, of which he had many. For as long as he could remember, he faithfully followed the rules of many common wives' tales, avoiding the underside of ladders, knocking on wood. Despite the fact that he did not believe in the underlying cosmic retribution. Not really. In addition to the colloquial ones, Blake added several unique superstitions of his own. Particularly, when it came to missions.

Satisfied with his less than thorough check of the house, Blake returned to the kitchen, opened the refrigerator, and surveyed its contents more thoroughly than he had the rest of the house. He selected a carton of orange juice, pulled a glass from the cupboard, and poured the juice until it reached the top of the glass. He shook the carton to gauge the weight of the sloshing liquid.

This wouldn't be worth putting back.

He drank from the carton, finishing the last of it.

He picked up his smartphone from the inductive charger, allowed the face-recognition software to unlock it, and swiped through the screen until he found the icon for the United Bank app.

Blake normally enjoyed being able to leave his phone at home while running or going to the gym. His smart watch was connected to the cellular network and allowed him to still receive calls, read texts, and listen to music. But with his bank cards malfunctioning, he wished he had taken his smartphone along this time.

He touched the icon and allowed the online banking application to load while he took a long gulp of juice. "Login Failed."

You've got to be kidding me! Is the whole thing down?

Blake manually keyed in his username and password. "Login Failed," the screen complained.

He searched for the United Bank customer service number, touched to accept the autodial, turned on the speaker mode, and left the phone on the island counter. After navigating a series of voice prompts, Blake was treated to a nondescript performance of

Beethoven's Ninth Symphony. He finished his juice and waited, tapping his fingers in syncopated rhythm.

Come on. Pick up the phone.

Blake's mind wandered. He thought about the last time he had seen Anja. About the guilt he had for pushing her away. About how he wanted to tell her he did it for her safety, for her well-being. He replayed how, when he saw her in the gym, he yearned to tell her he really did love her. That he had always loved her. That he always would.

Oh yeah, that would have gone over well. "Hey Jo, how've you been? It's been a while. By the way, you were the love of my life and I pushed you away because I was a clandestine operative putting you in danger simply for being associated with me. Oh, and I had no choice but to lie to you on a daily basis. Cheers."

Blake shook his head at the thought, as if trying to eject it through his ears. He brought his glass to his lips before realizing it was empty. As he set it back down, he caught the slightest whiff of his own sweat-driven stench. As if not content with the peripheral experience, he lifted his arm and buried his nose into his armpit.

Whoof! That's ripe.

Blake mashed the 'end' button on the phone, figuring his time would be better spent washing the foul odor off himself. He willfully deluded himself with the idea that there would be less of a queue if he called back in a few minutes.

He grabbed his phone and headed toward the stairs. He paused, reached into his pocket, pulled out Anja Kohler's business card, and stared at the back of it. At the personal cell phone number she wrote there.

He opened his phone and brought up the dialing screen. He stood at the base of the staircase, his intention to quickly grab a shower temporarily forgotten. His thumb hovered over the glowing numbers. He felt his body reacting to the thought of connecting with her again, if only by voice. His pulse quickened and slight perspira-

35

tion dampened his palms. It was as if he was caught in a mental tractor beam, trying to muster the strength to break free.

What the hell is wrong with me?

He dropped his hands to his sides and let out an audible sigh. It had been a long time since he was so affected. Dangerous situations, daring escapes, life-threatening injuries. These things had been commonplace for much of his adult life. Through it all, he considered himself a block of ice. But it only took the mere sight of a woman to turn him into a puddle.

He pocketed the phone and card and forced himself back on task.

Blake retreated to his bedroom, undressed as he walked to the bathroom, and turned on the shower. He flicked on a waterproof radio that was fastened to the shower wall by a large suction cup. It was an unwavering part of his routine. The preset talk-radio station served to maximize the otherwise mentally idle time by allowing him to catch up on the news of the day.

Blake's regimented day was purely of his own making. Retiring from government work and taking up a job writing code for a midsize web development firm had allowed him the flexibility to work remotely and set his own hours. He was required to attend a video-conference development meeting once a week but was otherwise free to structure his life however he saw fit. And how he saw fit was to abide by a rigid schedule.

The voice of Ed Glass, host of the Morning Drive Show, echoed off the hard tile walls.

"New information coming in at this hour of the hostage situation at IPFG," the radio squawked. "I'm being told sources close to one of the released hostages is reporting that several employees may have been injured or killed in the robbery attempt."

Blake hopped into the shower and turned up the volume to discern the words over the rushing water.

"Cynthia Dryer is on scene. Cynthia," the announcer segued.

The strained voice of the reporter cut in, struggling to enunciate over the background noise. "I'm standing about a hundred yards from the IPFG building. The whole vicinity has been cordoned off, and we're still seeing a lot of law enforcement personnel arriving. The police were evacuating people from the building about an hour ago, but we haven't seen many more civilians come out for the past thirty minutes. I spoke with several onlookers who reported hearing gun fire coming from inside. According to a relative of one of the released hostages, there may be as many as three civilian casualties. Also, sources say a police tactical team entered the building from the roof and may have shot and killed the five perpetrators. So far police are not commenting on whether they have taken anyone into custody, but, as of yet, no one out here has witnessed anyone being taken out in handcuffs. The good news is the police have announced the threat is over, and there is no danger to the public at this time."

While he listened, Blake visualized Ed Glass and Cynthia Dryer based on physical descriptors he had invented purely inside his mind. He made the mistake, once, of looking at their actual pictures on the show's website. They looked so unlike the imagined versions, his subconscious simply rejected the real images and opted to use the concocted ones instead.

"Cynthia," the announcer chimed in, "what do we know about the suspects?"

"Not a whole lot, Ed."

Blake switched the radio off and twisted the valve to stop the flow of water.

He got dressed and headed down the two flights of stairs toward the bottom level. It was time to go to work, and he was running late.

6

"My office is just down the hall," Reid said as he, Anja, and Harrison stepped off the elevator onto the fourth floor.

The hallway was lined with glass panels and doors tightly partitioning off various spaces. Despite the narrowness of the corridor and the over-ambitious floor plan, the use of glass walls gave the entire floor a bright, open feel.

As they moved down the corridor, Anja could see Wells in one of the rooms, sitting at a conference table with several other people. Anja knew a couple of them from the Bureau but didn't recognize the others. She considered trying to dart by the room to avoid getting bogged down by her boss, but there was no cover whatsoever. And it was already too late.

Oliver Wells motioned to her with his index finger pointed upward as his mouth continued forming words she could not hear through the sound-proof partitions. The gesture clearly conveyed that he wanted her to stay exactly where she was until he could finish his conversation.

"Go ahead and get started," Anja said to Harrison. "I'll fill in

Wells."

Harrison nodded as Reid began leading him further down the corridor.

Anja waited while Wells continued to speak with an older man, who Anja estimated to be in his sixties. Anja could not keep from noticing that the man was undeniably attractive for his age. His thick, well-manicured hair and sharp, chiseled nose and chin gave him a strong, distinguished air. His Brioni suit was expertly tailored, and Anja could not detect a single wrinkle in the lush fabric.

Wells bobbed his head in a series of exaggerated nods as he stood up from the table. The older man continued speaking to the rest of the group as Wells silently excused himself and moved to the door. Anja tried to read the lips of both men. She discovered this wasn't as easy a proposition as it first seemed.

"Who was that?" Wells asked as he ducked into the corridor, closing the door behind him. "And what's he doing up here?"

"One of the IPFG employees. He says he may be able to help us find out if the suspects were able to compromise their systems. Who is that?" Anja reciprocated, motioning to the well-dressed man, still engaged in an animated one-sided conversation.

"That, Agent Kohler, is Jacob Milburn. The President and CEO of IPFG Financial."

"He came here in person. Why? I mean, doesn't that seem unusual?"

Wells was already becoming perturbed by Anja's efforts to change the subject and reverse his mini-interrogation back on him.

"Mr. Milburn has offered resources to assist in the investigation and wanted to check on the well-being of his employees. In person. I'd say that's unusually gracious. Now, why don't you and Harrison get on identifying the suspects so we can start giving Mr. Milburn and his team some answers?"

Anja was not surprised by the redirection. She had become accustomed to Wells hastily doling out obvious or routine tasks, as if they were novel ideas that could only be formulated by a true mastermind. Tasks that could not possibly be delayed a single second longer, for no justifiable reason. Oftentimes, he had already assigned the task to another agent causing one of them to waste hours or even days on the fool's errand. In this case though, she agreed. Identifying the five subjects had to be her priority. *After* she finished with Reid.

"Look. Trust me on this. If all of this was carefully planned and executed for the purpose of getting access to a computer terminal, we must know why. If they've infected the computers with some kind of malicious software, there's no time to spare."

"Alright, Kohler. Hurry up. I'll let Milburn know what you're working on and try to buy some time on the IDs," Wells said as he swung open the heavy conference room door.

Milburn glanced at Wells and then at Anja. As he did, his eyes locked on to hers. He casually shifted his gaze down and up, as if taking a 3D scan of her dimensions. Moving back to her eyes, a confident smile appeared on his face.

Anja felt her face becoming flushed. She purposefully broke eye contact and hurried down the corridor to find Harrison and Reid.

With little difficulty, she found them in one of the two corner offices, situated at the end of the main corridor. Harrison was standing behind Reid, looking over his shoulder as the computer engineer rattled away at the keyboard.

"I did a comparison of the current state against the backup from just before the incident. Anything that was added, deleted, or changed would be readily apparent, but there's nothing suspicious. The only changes I can see are located in system files. Page files, log files, stuff like that. It's exactly as you would expect. The SHA256 hash values of the automatic backups from before and after the incident match exactly, meaning no pertinent files were compromised."

Anja was not exactly sure she could repeat what Reid said, verbatim, but she was confident she understood the gist of it. She let Reid continue without interruption.

"Maybe they were stealing information after all. Good news is, we capture every packet that passes through our routers and save it for twenty-four hours. I just have to locate the exact time the breach occurred, and I'll be able to inspect the traffic and determine if they sent anything out," Reid explained.

Anja joined Harrison, watching the computer screen over Reid's other shoulder as he scrolled through what appeared to be an infinite list of gibberish.

As Reid conjured screen after screen of information, Anja's mind momentarily wandered back to a time, many years prior, when Blake would show her lines of computer code and attempt to explain why he was having difficulties solving one problem or another. Inevitably, Blake would have an epiphany, mid-explanation, and thank her for the insight before retreating to his office to finish implementing the solution she inspired. She didn't actually understand any of it. Even in humoring him, she would freely admit that computer code was a foreign language to her. But Blake never seemed to care. He would say the one-sided conversation was just what he needed to approach the problem from a different angle. Rubber-ducking, he called it.

Anja let out a chuckle recalling the ridiculousness of the term. Wondering if her slight verbalization had betrayed her inattention, her mind snapped her back to the present. She looked at Harrison and Reid, embarrassed. Despite all that had happened and all that needed to be done, she could not put her ex-boyfriend out of her mind. Seeing him stirred something she had long since suppressed. But she would have to leave that for later.

"Okay, here it is," Reid said. "Yep. They definitely sent data out of the building. About two hundred gigabytes worth."

"What does that mean? I mean, is it significant? Do you know what they sent? What they were after?" Anja rattled off questions, not waiting for the answers.

"I don't know. There's no way to know. The connection was encrypted. The data in the packets is unreadable. I can only tell you that it seems like they were after a particular bit of information."

Anja tilted her head back in a physical manifestation of mental defeat. She hoped Reid would be able to generate a lead. Something that could point her to a possible motive. "Is there anything else you can tell us?"

"I can give you the IP address where they transferred the data to. Although I doubt it will be much use. There's no way a group like the Evangelists are going to leave a trail. At least not one a cop would be able to trace." Reid shot a skittish smile at the two FBI agents staring blankly back at him. "What? I'm just sayin'."

The glass door to the office flew open so forcefully, Anja was sure it would shatter. Jacob Milburn stood in the doorway.

"Enough," he said sharply. "Our CTO and VP of Digital Security are on the way here. I'd appreciate it if you would cease whatever it is you're doing here before you do any more damage."

Anja hardly recognized Milburn as the same man she had seen only a couple of minutes earlier. The charming veneer that previously intrigued her had peeled away to reveal a base layer of petulance. She looked to Reid, immediately sorry she put him in an undoubtedly uncomfortable position.

Only, Reid did not appear to be uncomfortable. His brow furrowed, slanting his eyebrows toward his nose. His irises pinned to the left in a distant stare. As if he was confused.

Wells instantly attempted to placate the man. "Mr. Milburn. I apologize. My agents were only trying to..."

"Agent Wells, spare me the apologies. Just keep your employees in check," Milburn snapped.

Anja felt her temper boiling up in her throat. The anger was not totally triggered by Milburn's condescending words. It came from the fact that Wells failed, once again, to have their backs.

"This is a crime scene, and with all due respect, my agents are authorized by a federal judge and the U.S. Attorney's Office to lock down and search the entire premises, including all digital media. We may allow anyone access to this facility, to whatever extent is deemed necessary, and for however long is required to ensure the integrity of the scene. Now, I'll have to ask you to leave the premises," is what he should have said. But Anja knew he would say nothing.

Anja noticed Reid's expression changed from one of contemplation to one of epiphany. His eyebrows raised and his eyes became as large as dinner plates.

"Mr. Milburn," Reid stuttered. "Of course, you are. I mean, I'm sorry sir. I was simply reviewing the network traffic logs. I didn't disturb anything. Actually, I noticed something peculiar you may be interested in."

Milburn raised his hand in a casual gesture that had the effect of silencing Reid. And everyone else in the room.

"Do you work for me, Mister...?" Milburn paused.

"Reid. Steven Reid. Yes. I'm a senior engineer on the GraphQL team, sir."

"Well, Mr. Reid. You're fired," Milburn said with no discernible inflection. He turned to the younger man who followed Milburn into the room like he was attached by a short, invisible line. He had black slicked-back hair and was holding an open leather-covered notebook, as if he were poised to jot down any thought Milburn might spontaneously utter. "McGovern, see Mr. Reid out," Milburn directed.

The room sank deeper into silence as Milburn turned and walked out of view, leaving McGovern to face the emotionally charged lash-out which would inevitably follow the rash order. But there was none. Reid just sat stunned and speechless.

"I'm sorry, Mr. Reid. You heard him," McGovern said, squeamishly.

"Harrison, Kohler. Downstairs, now," Wells barked, loud enough for Milburn to still hear him.

Anja pulled out her business card and placed it on the desk in front of Reid. She placed her hand on Reid's shoulder and said, simply, "Sorry."

Anja and Harrison walked down the corridor and rode the elevator to the ground level without saying a word.

As they exited the elevator and walked toward the front of the lobby, Harrison finally spoke.

"What in the hell was that?" he said.

"I have no idea, buddy." Anja's forehead was scrunched into rows of wrinkles by her raised eyebrows. "But I'm pretty sure this thing couldn't get any worse."

"I don't know about that, Agent Kohler," Kame Yamazaki said from about twenty feet away, standing over the body of one of the suspects. "There's something you've got to see."

Anja had been friends with Yamazaki, even before she started working as a civilian crime scene technician for the FBI. She insisted on calling Anja "Agent Kohler" while at work, even though Anja repeatedly told her not to. She let it go.

Anja and Harrison moved toward Yamazaki. Before the pair even reached her, the spectacle of what lay before them negated any need for Yamazaki to point out her findings. The masks of the five deceased men had been removed. From Anja's vantage point, it appeared to her as though the men did not possess faces at all.

Anja stopped five feet from the closest corpse. Without looking at Harrison, she reached to her left and grabbed his forearm, squeezing tightly. Anja's heart raced as she tried to make sense of the disturbing sight.

"Burned," Yamazaki said. "Face, hands. God knows what else. There are no discernible fingerprints, which means there's no way we're going to identify any one of them without a DNA hit."

Anja approached and crouched down next to one of the bodies. She examined the mottled, petrified skin that served as a counterfeit face.

"My god. His nose, lips, ears, all gone. If it weren't for the eyes, you wouldn't even be able to identify this as someone's face. I mean, it doesn't help that the top of his head is missing, but still. What happened to these guys?" Anja asked as she recovered from the initial shock.

"Are we even sure they're males?" Harrison asked.

"Yes. We've confirmed all five are male," Yamazaki answered.

Harrison decided not to ask how.

"Harrison," Anja said, standing. "We've got some work to do."

7

B   lake reached the bottom of the stairs and punched a
       passcode into a keypad on the wall next to a stainless-steel
       door. The mechanism was wholly unlike the consumer
grade deadbolt installed on the front door. This keypad triggered
large actuators built into the fortified wall, which slid all the way into
the thick metal door. This system was typically used in large vaults,
which was essentially Blake's home office.

As Blake pushed open the door, the sound of whirling fans
escaped. It had been building up by the door and waiting for
someone to release it.

Blake walked in and sat at his desk. He kept the desktop clear of
any clutter, leaving only a keyboard, mouse, and four 5K computer
monitors, lined up in a slight arc across a large rectangular desk.

He pushed the redial button on his phone's screen, navigated the
prompts by memory, and laid the speaker-enabled phone down on
the desk. He listened to a low fidelity rendition of Brahms while he
fired up the beast of a desktop computer and logged in.

He had this secure facility built while still working with the
Agency. He had outfitted it with a state-of-the-art climate control

system, air filtration system, and fire-suppression system. Inside, the room was appointed with some of the best computer equipment money could buy, as well as some that simply could not be bought.

Large enclosures, each containing a dozen rack servers, spanned the length of one wall. Two thin enclosures were mounted on an adjacent wall, each housing fifty graphics-processing units, connected to a custom motherboard, designed by Blake himself. The GPUs' architecture was such that it made them especially good at processing decryption algorithms. Used in parallel, the setup was capable of cracking passwords with ease.

Only three other living souls had ever seen the inside of the room after it had been built. Two of them were his former teammates, Fezz and Khat. The other was an installer. Blake had recently upgraded to dedicated fiber when it became available in his area. He was reluctant, but the promise of an extreme improvement in Internet bandwidth had forced his decision. Although the worker did comment about the sheer amount of equipment in the room, he did not show a deep interest. Blake told him he was running a small Internet company. The man seemed to be satisfied enough with that explanation.

The capability of his setup was beyond overkill for his new job of writing JavaScript code for web applications. The simplistic coding work was enjoyable enough and provided some extra cash flow. But Blake continued to maintain multiple pieces of severely complex, classified software, which he originally developed while working for the government.

He made a point to continually upgrade his software to take advantage of new advancements in processors and memory and try to keep up with the ever-changing paradigms of security and cryptology. Of course, Blake regularly provided these updates to his old colleagues, as a gesture of camaraderie.

Upgrading the software also meant constantly upgrading his equipment to allow him to run and test its functionality against real-world scenarios.

"Real-world scenarios." This was Blake's softened term for hacking actual live computer systems. He thought it a useful effort to keep his skills sharp and, by most measures, he had done just that.

Since becoming a civilian, he had accessed hundreds of supposedly secure systems. But he prided himself on never causing any damage, downtime, or trace of his presence. Blake was not a criminal and he despised those who used such skills and technical capability to cheat and steal. While he also was not a vigilante, he certainly didn't mind occasionally giving the so-called "black hats" a taste of their own medicine.

"United Bank, how may I help you?" A woman said, finally cutting into the elevator music.

"Hi. My name is Blake Brier, and I need to check on my account. There's something wrong with my debit and credit cards, maybe a fraud alert? Your website is down so I haven't been able to check," Blake explained.

"Okay. Mr. Brier, can I have your account number and access code?"

Blake provided the information and waited for several seconds while the woman loudly clicked the keys of a keyboard.

"I don't show any such account number. Can you give it to me again?"

Blake complied, reading the numbers verbatim.

"Sorry sir, we don't have that account number. Are you sure you called the correct bank?"

"Yes, I'm sure. I've had accounts with you for twenty years. Can you look me up by name?" He suggested.

"Okay. Brier. No, sorry, I don't have any accounts under that name," the woman said in an increasingly condescending tone. "Is there anything else I can do for you?"

Blake considered how to answer the question but decided most of the options were too harsh for the undeserving messenger. He went with "No. Thanks."

Blake hung up the phone and leaned back in his chair. He

wanted to be able to handle this through the standard channels. Like a normal person. But the light from the screens, connected to the massive cluster of computers, radiated on his face as if inviting him in. Giving him permission. He had already accessed the United Bank's servers once before. As an exercise. Accessing it again would take little effort now that he was familiar with the exploit and had already done the heavy lifting. And it wouldn't hurt to do a little bit of harmless investigation.

Blake launched a virtual machine running Kali Linux and accessed a terminal window. He typed in the commands and parameters needed to run the attack. His fingers flew across the keyboard, punctuated by a hard tap of the enter key.

He watched the flurry of console output with complete confidence the communication would be untraceable. Thanks to Blake's software, the traffic, encrypted using still-classified algorithms, would first pass through the TOR network, obfuscating the origin IP address through a series of proxies. The encrypted packets would then hit an exit node, traverse the regular Internet where they would pass through six clandestine data centers, located in various locations around the world. The encrypted payload would be decrypted in six separate stages, ultimately being re-encrypted with a standard scheme before being forwarded to the target. By the time the endpoint was reached, the origin would be untraceable.

The lines of output abruptly stopped, leaving an open SSH prompt. The flashing cursor beckoned him. Commands run at this prompt would be interpreted by the target system itself. As if he were physically sitting at a keyboard in United Bank's data center.

Before he could touch the keyboard, the characters "vim" appeared, one by one, at the prompt. The VIM text editor filled the terminal window. Someone was sharing control of his connection.

Not possible.

Blake racked his brain but could not come up with even the faintest beginnings of how this was remotely possible. Even if someone were physically sitting at the computer, logging in to the compromised account would only spawn a new shell. This was something else, a complete hijacking of the same encrypted connection.

More characters appeared on the screen.

"Mr. Brier."

The mention of his name made Blake's stomach sink. His senses heightened by a quick injection of adrenalin. His jaw tightened and his eyes narrowed.

So, you want to play. Is that it?

"Who is this?" Blake typed, just below the original message.

"You can call me Bob--" the cursor flashed "--if you would like."

"Who is Mr. Brier? This is Randy." Blake wrote, as he brought up another shell and furiously typed commands, trying desperately to glean some information about the methods and origin of the intruder.

"Please, Mr. Brier. I know more about you than you know about yourself. We only have a few moments. Wouldn't you like your money back? That's why you are here, is it not?"

My money? Could it be that this guy stole my money, erased all record of my twenty-year banking history, hacked an incredibly secure remote connection in a way that isn't even theoretically possible, and now wants me to call him fucking Bob?

"Yes, Bob. Now that you mention it, I would like it back. Bob." Blake typed out the letters with heavy-handed strokes, trying with all his might to keep his composure.

"Don't worry, it's safe and sound. All one hundred ninety-four thousand six hundred twenty-two dollars, and fifteen cents," Bob said, proving his veracity.

"Why don't we cut through the BS. What do you want?" Blake typed.

"Your help," Bob wrote.

Blake stopped splitting his attention between tasks. He had already begun writing a script to deliver a payload to Bob's terminal that he hoped would send enough data back to later analyze and determine the origin of Bob's connection. But he realized he probably would not have anywhere near enough time to execute his plan. And Bob's statement intrigued him.

"Help with what?" Blake typed.

The characters slowly appeared, one after another. "I-P-F-G."

Oh lord. Don't tell me this crazy bastard is involved in this IPFG thing.

"What about it?" Blake replied.

"Please, Mr. Brier. I am out of time. Your skill set and connections are perfectly suited to intervene in this matter. It is important. Very important. The FBI, the police, no one realizes what this is really about. You will be contacted. I only ask you to keep an open mind."

Blake watched as the characters continued to appear in rapid succession.

"As for your bank accounts, you will find your funds have been safely transferred here." The typing paused, and then two long strings of characters appeared at once. A Bitcoin address and private key.

The cursor jumped to a new line. Bob wrote, "It's about Bitcoin. That's what the police and FBI are missing. There are powerful people involved. Very resourceful people. Do not underestimate them."

The connection terminated. And with it, any reasonable chance of figuring out Bob's identity.

Blake immediately opened the Bitcoin blockchain and searched for the address he was given.

It was all there. Every penny.

8

Aaron Hosier wore no expression as he knelt on the cold stone floor, cloaked in a black wool cape and hood. His lack of outward emotion concealed the pride and sense of fulfillment that invisibly oozed from his pores.

He had never particularly liked himself. And he fully believed no one would miss him if he were to disappear off the face of the earth. Even kneeling there in anticipation, he could not recall a single moment in his twenty years when he felt content. When he felt like he belonged. Until today. The day Aaron Hosier would cease to exist.

Growing up in Massachusetts, Aaron was always a loner. Like many of his classmates, his parents had been divorced since before he could remember. Raised by a single mother, their lives were not without struggle. But no more so than anyone else he knew. He never complained or wished for wealth, happiness, or success. He was perfectly apathetic.

As apathy turned to reclusion, Aaron would spend his days and nights in his room, often lit only by the light emitted from his computer monitor. Out of disconnected curiosity, he would experiment with ways to connect to the outside world anonymously. He joined chat groups and forums where he learned about phishing, cracking, and spoofing. He met coders and hackers who provided him with digital versions of textbooks and manuals. He practiced around the clock and would share his successes with others who he knew only by handle or screen name. His only friends in the world were invisible. And so was he.

By the time he was eighteen years old, he was making a modest living by stealing information, generating forged documents, and scamming the unsuspecting masses. In order to operate with anonymity, he used cryptocurrency, not only to receive payment, but also to acquire just about anything he needed. He found the concept to be beautiful. So perfectly simplistic.

A growing disdain for the government's transparent efforts to maintain control over its citizens by undermining and vilifying cryptocurrency eventually morphed into an obsession. An obsession that would have unquestionably led to his own destruction if it had not been for Metus.

Aaron began attacking financial institutions and government agencies he believed were working against the decentralization of finance for their own gain. As the attacks became more brazen and the accompanying rhetoric more raucous, Aaron began attracting the attention of the authorities. Unbeknownst to Aaron, the FBI had successfully identified him and obtained approval for an operation that would have led to his arrest and a raid of his home.

Metus had intercepted the details of the operation and sent several of his disciples to retrieve Aaron and provide him a safe place to hide from the impending retribution. Aaron was initially skeptical. Indeed, the masked disciples were forced to blindfold, gag, and bind Aaron's hands and feet to carry out the rescue, but it was for his own good.

The fragrance of the incense filling the stone room brought back the memory of when he met Metus in person for the first time. He was already familiar with the name. Hell, everyone in Aaron's online circle of cohorts knew the handle. But as far as Aaron knew, no one had ever actually set eyes on him in the flesh.

Metus was a legend. An apparition. And as the leader of the most prolific hacktivist group in history, he was, to Aaron, a hero. Better yet, a god.

Aaron had been brought to this room, tied to a chair, and left for hours to listen to the echoes of his own screams for help bounce off the bare stone. The maddening silence was broken by the creaking of a door and the soft steps of his captor approaching him.

The man removed his blindfold and spoke softly. "Do you know who I am?" he asked.

Aaron's eyes had adjusted to the darkness of the blindfold. The light of four torches, mounted on the four walls of the room, lit up the scene like the sun. In front of him stood a terrifying sight.

The slight, barefooted man, wearing only a pair of loose pants, was hideously deformed. His hairless head and body were marred by reddened scars, contrasting against the pasty white color of the smoother areas of his skin. His nose and ears looked like melted mounds of flesh. But his eyes, peering out from inside the monster, conveyed a peaceful knowingness.

Aaron should have been frightened. Disgusted, at least. Instead, he felt welcomed. And he thought the grotesque figure before him was the most beautiful thing he had ever seen.

"You're Metus," Aaron managed to say.

Metus smiled. He freed Aaron from his bindings and sat facing him. Aaron never considered trying to flee or fight. He was mesmerized, as if he really were in the presence of an apparition. The two men talked for hours. Metus explained how he had been chosen by God to lead the faithful against the tyranny of greed, why he had chosen the name Metus, and how he had been watching Aaron closely, waiting for the right time to bring him into the fold. He told Aaron of the divine mission of the Cryptocurrency Evangelist Army and of the plan God had for him. By the end of the long night, Aaron resolved that he would never return to his old life.

In the months that followed, Aaron lived and worked with the disciples, each as physically grotesque as their leader. Instead of names, he knew them only by their given numbers. He realized they must have once had names, had lives outside the faith, but could not imagine any of them as individuals. They were devout, they were committed, and they were extremely skilled at cyber-mayhem. But, most importantly, they were nobody.

Now, giving himself over completely to the cause. To the order. To God. He was not convinced that Metus was merely a prophet, as the disciples believed him to be. Aaron truly believed he was an angel.

A group of faceless figures, clad in the same heavy cloaks, filed into the room, and encircled him. The low, melodic chanting of the group was intoxicating. A tingle traveled around Aaron's scalp and down his spine, causing his body to shiver. Then, he heard the voice of an angel.

"God has spoken to me, my son," Metus bellowed. "In his eyes, you have proven yourself worthy. Do you now denounce your name and give yourself unconditionally to the Lord?"

"I do," Aaron replied.

"And do you swear undying loyalty to your brethren, the cause, and to me, as the hand of God's will?" Metus continued.

"Yes, I do," he said.

"And do you understand the penalty for disloyalty and treachery, as commanded to me by God, is death?"

"I understand," Aaron replied.

"Then it shall be done," Metus finished. He motioned to the group surrounding Aaron.

Eight disciples closed in upon Aaron Hosier, pulling the cloak from his shoulders and exposing his bare torso. One of the disciples guided Aaron backwards until he laid flat on his back, arms outstretched to the sides. Four of the disciples straddled him, one on each leg and one on each arm, pinning him to the ground. A fifth held the back of his head.

Metus approached, leaned down, and with his thumb, drew the sign of the cross on Aaron's forehead.

Aaron's eyes were as wide as saucers as he watched his Prophet and Savior spark the propane torch. Blue and yellow flames raged from the metal nozzle. Aaron's body began to shake and his arms and legs instinctively tried to retract. The weight of the five men prevented him from moving more than a few inches in any direction.

As Metus drew the flame toward Aaron, he proclaimed, "Aaron Hosier is dead. Born from fire is a soldier. Number one-three."

"Wait!" was the last word Soldier Thirteen would utter before his ability to form words was swallowed by primal screams.

9

Anja straightened her back to better see Harrison's mouth over the divider that separated her desk from his. She attempted to read his lips to fill in the words she was losing due to the background noise in the busy office. The walls of the dividers were covered with foam and fabric, designed to allow the use of pushpins to post notes. The plush box that contained her on three sides conspired with the commercial carpeting to absorb everything Harrison was saying to her.

"I didn't catch that," Anja admitted.

"I said, we acquired the video footage from IPFG. Do you want to watch it with me?" Harrison repeated.

"Sure." Anja got up and walked around the row of eight cubicles. She pulled up a chair next to Harrison, who had already queued up the video on his computer. Anja's eye was caught by the scaly black-and-gray pattern of Harrison's pointed shoes.

"Are you wearing cowboy boots?" she asked.

"Yeah. So? Where I'm from, cowboy boots are the most important part of the wardrobe," he said.

"You're from Massachusetts," Anja rebutted.

"Ah. I grew up in Mass, but I was *born* in San Antonio," he said, as if he had instantly won the argument with his statement.

Anja shook her head. "Just start the thing."

Harrison clicked play and the two watched the entire event unfold from the moment the five men approached the building to the time SWAT entered the lobby.

Anja held a yellow legal pad to notate the times of each significant event for her forthcoming case report. The murder of the tellers, the murder of the IT employee, the release of the hostages. Anja stared down at her paper.

"Let me ask you something," Anja said. She continued without waiting for a response. "Do you think they did that to themselves? Burned themselves, I mean. Maybe there were drastic measures to prevent authorities from identifying them. Maybe it was to make a point of some kind. Maybe they were all in an accident. A botched bombing attempt or something. But what are the chances they would all be disfigured in the same way, losing all facial features. All fingerprints. Do all the CEA members look like that? I can't say I've ever seen one before, have you?"

Harrison waited as if he were trying to determine if Anja was finished.

"I'd never even heard of them before this morning," he said.

"I have," said Agent Rory Planc, popping his head up from the cubicle adjacent to Harrison.

Harrison leaned in toward Anja. "He's got no problem hearing me," he said. A wry smile on his face.

"When I was assigned to the New York office," Planc continued. "Three of these yahoos stole the cash from a Costco store one of them worked at. A good amount too. Can't remember exactly but it was probably around thirty thousand dollars. Anyway, the three of them put on those masks and dumped the cash off the top of a building at Washington Park. Caused mayhem on the street. All three were arrested by NYPD but we were called in because of the connection to the so-called cyber-terrorism group."

"I take it they weren't burnt beyond recognition," Anja said.

"Nope. They were punk kids. Mommy and Daddy weren't paying enough attention to them or something. They admitted they were part of the CEA and claimed the stunt was orchestrated by some other super-hacker. They didn't know his real name, just his corny-ass hacker name. I can't remember what it was. Long story short, we never ended up getting any useful information from them. But to answer your question, no, they weren't burned up."

Having said his piece, the agent sank down into his chair, out of view.

"Our suspects could be copycats. That's possible, right? Maybe they're wearing the masks, but don't actually have any affiliation with the group," Anja said.

"Whoever they're with, my concern is how many more of them there are. And whether this is going to happen again soon," Harrison said.

"What we need, "Anja interjected, "is to find out what they wanted. What did they copy from that computer? If we find that out, we have a motive. If we have a motive, we have a much better shot at predicting their next move."

Anja's ringtone, a clip of a guitar chord being strummed, sounded from her own cubicle. Instead of making the trip around the long row of cubicles, which would have most likely caused her to miss the call, Anja put one knee on Harrison's desk and hoisted herself upward. Just enough to lean her body over the divider and reach her phone. She pulled it back and glanced at the incoming number on the screen. She didn't recognize it.

She swiped her finger across the screen to accept the call.

"Agent Kohler," she said, walking away from Harrison, toward the door leading from the office into the main second-floor hallway.

"Hi Jo, it's Blake."

"Blake. Hi," Anja replied, "sorry, I didn't recognize the number."

"Yeah. I had to change it a while back. This is my cell so you can save the contact if you want." He paused. "Is this a bad time?"

"No. It's fine. I needed to take a break. Clear my head. The day's gone downhill since I saw you at the gym," she said.

"Oh. I'm sorry to bother you, but..."

"No. Please. No bother," Anja cut in emphatically. She winced at the way the words came out so enthusiastically.

"Well, I know you're busy. I was wondering, do you know who is working on that IPFG attack?" he asked.

Anja chuckled. "Sure do." She paused. "Me. Why?"

"Perfect," Blake said, his tone relaying his relief at the news. "So, I had contact with someone a little while ago. I'll tell you about that later. I don't know a whole lot about what happened at the bank, but this person suggested it may have something to do with Bitcoin. You may already know that, but the person seemed to think the FBI is on the wrong track."

"That's not a stretch. Our bad guys were from a group called the Evangelists. Apparently, their whole deal has to do with Bitcoin. Well, cryptocurrency in general. The group's involvement has pretty much leaked out at this point. Your friend probably saw it on the news," Anja said.

"Maybe. Just figured I'd let someone know," he replied.

"No. Thanks. I'm glad you called. To be honest, this thing is a little over my head. I mean, it's definitely not your typical bank robbery."

"I was also thinking," Blake said, making his best attempt at laying on the charm. "I'm pretty familiar with this group and I have been known to dabble in computing."

Anja laughed at the understatement.

"If you were to, say, meet me for lunch, I could answer any questions you might have about Bitcoin, the Evangelists, computer stuff, whatever. And you've gotta eat, right?" Blake said.

Anja raised her fingertips to her mouth to hide the wide beaming smile, even though no one was nearby to see it.

"In the interest of furthering my investigation, of course. How could I say no?" she responded.

"Great. How about Alfie's? In an hour," he suggested.

"Make it two hours," she countered.

"Two it is. I'll tell you the rest of the story when we meet. See you there," he said.

"See you there," she replied, ending the call.

Anja fought with the muscles in her face, attempting to force a neutral expression. Only to lose the battle to the involuntary smile once again. As flirtatious as the conversation had become, she found herself hoping she didn't misread it. Maybe Blake was just reaching out to provide some information he thought would be useful. Maybe he wanted to see if he could be of some help.

Anja considered Blake to be one of the smartest people she had ever known. He had always been an expert problem-solver and was keenly perceptive about world affairs and geopolitics. He had a knack for reading people. And, when it came to computers, he was a genius. Considering what she knew about the case so far, Blake would be an extremely helpful resource.

Anja entered the office and swiftly took up her position next to Harrison and grabbed her notepad.

"Who was that?" Harrison asked.

"Just an old friend," she said. "Now, where were we?"

10

Blake arrived twenty minutes before he expected Anja to arrive. The popular deli-style restaurant-known for its famous corned beef sandwich- was almost always filled to capacity in the afternoon.

Blake stood by the register for ten minutes, surveying the four small tables and four booths, trying to gauge which diners were preparing to leave.

A couple, seated at a booth, began scooting out of the bench seats. To prevent a squabble with several people who came in right behind him, Blake quickly moved to the booth and sat, claiming his rightful spot in line. Blake thought it fortunate to get a booth because it offered a bit more privacy than the exposed tables. While the place was not ideal for a business meeting, it had once been his and Anja's favorite spot.

Worth the trade-off.

The waitress quickly arrived to grab the bills left for her by the last patrons. She cleared the dishes, visibly put off by not being allowed to clean the table before Blake sat down.

"I'll be right back to wipe this down," she said, hooking a hanging strand of hair behind her ear.

"No worries," Blake said. "I'm still waiting for someone."

The young woman nodded and retreated behind the counter which separated the kitchen from the tiny dining area.

Blake was not prepared earlier that morning. Anja's presence had completely caught him off guard. Evidence of his waning diligence. The dulling of situational awareness that came with civilian life. But he would be ready now. Prepared to absorb every morsel of Anja's company.

He smoothed the fabric of his off-white button-down shirt, making sure it was tucked in neatly. He adjusted the Submariner watch on his wrist. Busywork.

Prior to missions, Blake always found himself touching each piece of equipment that was strapped to him multiple times. A tactile checklist performed in the same order each time. The process offered a peace of mind that nothing was forgotten. But it was about the ritual. Like a prize fighter about to step into the ring, peering out from under a large silk hood, bouncing and dancing and punching at the air. A signal to the mind of a singular purpose.

Blake checked himself again.

Here we go.

The waitress wiped the table and went off to retrieve the black coffee Blake ordered. Blake looked around at the kitschy nineteen-sixties signs, toys, and artwork that adorned the place. It brought back memories.

Blake saw Anja the moment she opened the door. Her tall, slender frame was backlit by the mid-afternoon sun shining through the glass door at a shallow angle. The glow made her blonde hair look like fire. She was stunning, as always.

He stood as she made her way to the booth and sat down.

"Glad you made it," Blake said.

"Glad I was able to break free. I told my partner Harrison I had to run home for a few minutes. He's covering for me with Wells."

Anja looked around at the interior of the restaurant, which had not changed in the slightest over the last ten years.

"God, almost forgot about this place. It used to be my favorite. Remember when you dumped a whole milkshake in your lap? I think we were sitting in this booth," she said.

"I remember," he said.

What Blake remembered was the look on Anja's face. A second of surprise quickly transformed into a huge grin and a loud burst of laughter. Blake could not help but laugh as well. He laughed so hard he got a cramp in his abdomen. They both did. It was the kind of laugh that only happens on rare occasions and only under perfect conditions. Recalling that day, he realized he probably hadn't laughed like that since.

"So, I'm assuming you're still doing the computer thing. Still with Booz?" Anja asked.

When Blake met Anja, he had already been working for the CIA for four years. He was stationed in Stuttgart, Germany, and Anja was staying with her parents who moved back from the United States when Anja graduated from high school. His official cover story was that he was working for the contractor Booz Allen Hamilton, programming unmanned aerial vehicles. A story that persisted upon moving back to the States.

"Nope. Retired. Now I work from home for a web development company. A lot has changed," he said.

Man, is that an understatement.

Blake considered just laying the truth on her. All at once. After all, he was a civilian now and it probably no longer mattered. But it was not the time or place.

"That's great, Blake. Seems like you're doing well."

"How about you, Jo? I mean, I know you're still going strong with the Bureau and all. I noticed you aren't wearing a ring. I thought you'd be married with four or five kids by now," he joked.

"You're actually close. My husband Jonathan and I have three. I don't wear my rings while I'm working. Gives away too much personal information, you know?" she said.

Blake's face blanched and he wanted to smack himself for the assumption. He paused for several seconds trying to come up with words.

"I'm kidding," she said, finally letting him off the hook. "I've never been married. I was close once. I mean after you. But it didn't work out. The story of my life."

Blake made a playful groan and chuckled at the gag. Selfishly, he was relieved her initial statement was not true, convincing as it was.

"Let me tell you a little more about this case, maybe you can shed light on a few things," she said.

Blake noticed the slightest hint of a German accent. Only detectable when she said certain words. Although she was born in the United States, she had attended several years of primary school in Stuttgart. Blake used to enjoy trying to speak with her in German. While he achieved a rudimentary command of the German language during his time overseas, he could never keep up with Anja when she started rattling on.

"Do you folks know what you want?" the waitress interrupted.

"I'll have the works," she said, without hesitation. "And a water, please."

The famous open-faced corned beef sandwich, piled with coleslaw and French fries, was obligatory.

"I'll have the same," he followed.

The waitress collected the untouched menus and walked away.

"Okay. Fill me in," he said.

"So, here's the gist. Five guys take over the bank. They're wearing these white plastic masks. The masks are identical, but they each had a different variation of green paint around the eyes, like green blood or tears. We've confirmed the masks are associated with the CEA. Then the men deliberately kill several bank employees, access a computer system for several minutes, and all five commit suicide, simultaneously," she explained. "And I hope it goes without saying, all of this stays between us. I really shouldn't be talking about the details while the investigation is ongoing."

"Of course," Blake said. "I'm familiar with the masks you're talking about. From what I've read, the green blood is supposed to represent greed. You know, the seven deadly sins and all that. There are a lot of religious undertones in the disseminated propaganda. Apparently, the Evangelists believe the government and big banks are agents of the devil. They claim they are doing God's work by interfering in the operations of both. I've even seen them refer to themselves as God's army. There's a central figure that is mentioned quite a bit. A sort of prophet the followers call Metus."

Anja replied, "It seemed pretty clear from the name *Cryptocurrency Evangelist Army*, and from what we've gathered online, their main mission has to do with spreading cryptocurrency and working against those who are working against it. Is that not the case?"

"That's absolutely correct. And they're not completely off-base about the government or the banking industry. Both have been trying to prevent the proliferation of cryptocurrency since its invention. Efforts to pass laws and regulations to limit the usefulness of cryptocurrency and put its exchanges out of business have ramped up since Bitcoin's meteoric rise in value."

"I've heard of Bitcoin, but to be honest, I don't really know what it is or how the whole thing works. Why does there seem to be so much contention? And why do the banks or the government even care?"

"I'll try to break it down for you, but you're going to have to stick with me for a few minutes. It can be a bit difficult to follow," he warned.

"I'm listening," she said.

"In 2008, a mysterious, unidentified person, who goes by the name of Satoshi Nakamoto, invented blockchain technology to be used as the backbone for the first of many cryptocurrencies, Bitcoin. In simple terms, a blockchain is a public ledger that can record transactions. In this case, Bitcoin transactions. Transactions are organized into a block and that block is run through a hashing algorithm. The algorithm is called SHA256. This means the entire block is fed into the algorithm and a 256-bit number is spit out. The next block in the chain contains more transactions plus the hash value of the previous block, and so on."

"So, each block is tied to the next?" Anja asked, indicating she was following along.

"Yes. Because if something in the first block changed, so would its hash value. Because the second block contains the first hash, the hash value of the second block would be wrong and so on, right up the line. This is how one can be sure a blockchain is accurate. It would be extremely obvious if someone were to tamper with it," he said.

"I get that. But couldn't you change something and just rehash every block, one by one?" she asked.

" Here's the genius of blockchains. In addition to the transactions and hash of the previous block, a random number is also included. It's called a nonce. When hashing the block, the goal is to end up with a hash value that starts with a certain number of zeros. This is easier said than done. The computer verifying the block has to insert a random value, hash the block, and then check the result for the required number of zeros. If the result does not meet the requirement, a new random number is chosen, and the process continues over and over again, making the process computationally difficult, and therefore time-consuming."

"Who does these verifications? If no one knows who invented this, who's in charge of verifying the blocks?" Anja said.

Blake noticed Anja had begun to squint. An unconscious quirk that had always shown up when she was trying to concentrate. He had always found it endearing. This moment was no different.

"Anyone. Anyone with a fast-enough computer system can eventually solve the problem. Can pick the right random number to get a hash value with the right characteristics. The reward for this feat is an amount of Bitcoin. Not someone else's Bitcoin. Brand new Bitcoin. This is called mining. I'm sure you've heard of mining Bitcoin before, right?" Blake asked.

"Yes, I just never understood what it meant," she admitted.

"The problem is, once someone beats you to it, the block is submitted to the network and, once the solution is verified, it becomes a permanent part of the chain. Now, the next block has to include the hash of the recently accepted block and the miners have to start over with a new set of transactions. There's a little more complexity but that's the gist of how double spending is prevented. Because to change something in the chain, you'd have to mine a new block after also resolving the hash problem for each and every block following the change. All before someone else could solve the problem once. And even then, the new chain would be rejected because many of the nodes would recognize the new chain as fraudulent," he explained.

"Ingenious," Anja said. "I can understand why the financial industry would want to squash it. If it caught on, it would be just like a global cash economy."

"Exactly. And Bitcoin wasn't just an experiment in cryptography. Many believe, just as the CEA does, it was built specifically to combat the powerful and corrupt financial industry. In the first block, called the Genesis block, Nakamoto embedded the words: *The Times 03/Jan/2009 Chancellor on brink of second bailout for bank.* It refers to an article in the London newspaper that day. The inclusion of that headline is a pretty obvious message. In the scheme of things, if this Metus is a prophet, Nakamoto would be the Messiah."

"I can't believe that after all this time, no one knows who this Nakamoto is."

"There's been a lot of speculation over the years, but nothing certain. Most, if not all, of the coin presumably mined by Nakamoto has gone unspent. Which is amazing because, if he's alive, he's sitting on an absolute fortune."

"How do they know which bitcoins belong to Nakamoto if the blockchain is anonymous? I mean, I know we're off on a bit of a tangent but this is fascinating. I'm just curious," she said.

"The answer is pretty technical. It has to do with the way bytes are arranged on the original mining system and something called *extraNonce*. That's not important. Let's just say it's safe to assume that many of the original coins were mined by Nakamoto," he said.

Anja's phone began rumbling on the table. She accepted the call and put the phone to her ear.

"Go ahead," she said, her voice stern. "Okay, yes, I'll be back in a few. Thanks." She ended the call.

"Sorry Blake, I've gotta run, they need me back at the office."

Anja waved to the waitress. Capturing her attention, Anja spoke across the restaurant.

"Would you wrap mine to go? Sorry," she said.

"It's not the same when it gets cold," Blake said. Advice Anja used to impart on him when he would bring home takeout.

"I know. I know." She paused. "I was actually going to buy some bitcoin when the market was blowing up, but I never got around to figuring out how to do it," Anja said.

"Funny you should say that, because I am a recently proud owner of a whole lot of it," he said.

Anja looked at Blake in silence as if waiting for him to finish his thought.

"The source I was telling you about. It wasn't exactly a source as much as a maniacal genius who erased my entire banking history and, for some reason replaced my bank account balance with bitcoin," Blake said.

"Are you kidding me?" Anja said. Blake could see in her expression that she was skeptical he was setting her up for a punchline.

"I'm not kidding, Jo. Weirdest thing. I immediately moved the bitcoin to a paper wallet so it's safe. I've had a hell of a time finding a place I can withdraw cash, and then I found out I can only withdraw three hundred dollars at a time."

"Did you report it? That's a serious crime, Blake."

"Not yet. But I'll handle it. Somebody's playing games. I don't mind a good game now and then," he joked. "What he said though, that the FBI was on the wrong track. It's peculiar."

The waitress placed an overflowing plate in front of Blake and a Styrofoam container in front of Anja. Anja reached into her purse.

"It's on me," Blake said.

Anja paused. "Thank you."

"Hopefully, they take Bitcoin," he said with a wide grin.

"It's been great to see you. I really appreciate the info," she said, standing up from the table.

"Listen, Jo. There are some things I want to explain. Things I've wanted you to know for many years. I think it's time you knew. If you would give me that opportunity."

"Of course," she said. There was a genuine quality to her voice. "But I understand. There's no need to."

"Trust me, Jo. It'll make sense later," he said.

"Okay. I'll give you a call once I can get a handle on this case."

Blake watched as Anja walked away. He sat back with his arms outstretched on the back of the booth seat and allowed his head to fall back and rest against the top of the seat-back.

After a moment, he looked at the pile of corned beef on his plate, stood up, dropped a hundred-dollar bill on the table, and headed for the door.

11

Blake sat back in his beloved Herman Miller chair and stared past the empty Google search bar in the center of his screen. He could probably trace back most of the most harrowing missions to a similar blank input field. A simple search, a step over the edge of a deep well. Swinging from branch to branch with increasing velocity, he would allow the ideas to flow through him, from one link to another, until he saw it. His attack vector. It never ceased to amaze him how much information he could compile from readily available, public information.

Gotta start somewhere.

Blake typed, "Cryptocurrency Evangelist Army OR (CEA AND hack)," and clicked the Search button.

Down the rabbit hole we go.

He scrolled through pages of articles and social media posts related to the IPFG robbery.

"Cryptocurrency Evangelist Army OR (CEA AND hack) - IPFG." He refined the query to exclude the trending event from the results.

For forty-five minutes, Blake skimmed the content of dozens of sites until he landed on an article titled, "50 Most Notorious Hackers."

Hackers my ass.

Blake hated the use of the term "hacker" in this context. As he saw it, a true hacker is an expert programmer who uses computing to solve difficult problems in elegant ways. The media's use of the term had regressed into describing anyone who maliciously accessed information they were not supposed to have.

It was not the obligatory blurbs about Kevin Mitnick or Albert Gonzalez that interested Blake. It was number forty-seven. An unknown person using the moniker "PH4N7oM."

The article explained that, in 2017, a security flaw in the University of Virginia's network was exploited, allowing hackers to gain access and modify admission records. Over fifteen hundred students, all of whom had taken out student loans, were flagged as having received scholarship money. The modification triggered the automated system to refund the bank, which negated the balances on most loans. Initially, the school released a statement attributing the issue to a glitch in the software. In response, a Reddit user, PH4N7oM, wrote a post on the site claiming responsibility and detailing how it was accomplished. The last line of the post read, "Can you feel us? We are the righteous. We are CEA. We are salvation."

PH4N7oM. Phantom indeed.

Blake searched for the original Reddit post and read it several times. *If this Phantom was connected,* he thought, *he may have some useful information.* Blake considered reaching out and attempting to slowly gain the trust of his target. He could concoct a new online identity and build a footprint by spewing anti-establishment opinions over social media channels for several months. Or he could pull off a similar intrusion, hopefully bringing Phantom to him. In the end, he concluded that a long con would be too much time to invest in a possible dead end. Instead, he banked on the suspicion that there was one person Phantom was likely to blindly trust.

Blake searched the Reddit user-base for the usernames "Metus" and "M3TU5." No direct matches. He was not surprised. The figurehead of the CEA, if he existed at all, had never appeared in a public forum, on social media, or had otherwise never directly released a statement. While the handle appeared in countless sources, no one ever claimed to have seen or spoken to him, or her. Many experts believed Metus was a ghost. An idea generated by the factory of idealism and teenage angst.

Blake secured the username "M3TU5" and logged in.

Step one.

He opened a file viewer and searched his archive for a PDF document he created for a mission several years prior. This document was the payload for a phishing attack and contained a single embedded video file. The video itself was nothing more than a clip from an old "Ren and Stimpy" cartoon, but the real payload was a Python script that used the browser's video plugin to run on the target's system. There were only two caveats. One was that the script could not gain root permissions, which would not be an issue in this case. The other was that the target needed to have a Python interpreter installed. That was almost guaranteed to be the case.

The trick would be getting a paranoid hacker to open an unsolicited file from a ghost who opened an account ten minutes prior. For that, Blake would have to rely on the three human hacking tools: laziness, curiosity, and ambition. Phantom's response to the school's statement showed a need to take credit. Assuming Phantom never communicated with Metus directly, ghost or not, the curiosity of what the file contained would be crushing when put up against missing an opportunity to be noticed. To be let in. On the other hand, Phantom could be the head of the organization and smell a rat immediately. The way Blake saw it, he had nothing to lose.

Blake changed the text of the PDF to read, "We are salvation," and attached it to a private message. In the body of the message he wrote, "The revolution is now. Will you stand with me?"

Send.

Step two.

Blake took a sip of coffee, opened the browser, and began to search for another target. Another vector.

In less than one minute, files began appearing on the remote file share, a sure sign the PDF had been opened.

You dummy. Blake smiled at the thought of the confusion the cartoon clip must have caused.

The script's objective was to copy key files, if present, that could be used to locate the user. The files Blake was receiving were from phone backup archives stored on Phantom's hard drive. One of the files was an SQLite database used to log frequently visited locations. Blake copied the list of coordinates into a software application that resolved physical addresses from GPS data. Blake held his breath as the list populated and grouped the addresses together. One address stood out with ten times the amount of entries as the next most frequent location. A residential address.

Blake sometimes wondered if the public would ever have the capacity to truly understand how exposed they had become. In the digital age, advancements in technology moved faster and faster. More critically, these advancements were being adopted by the everyday citizens at a rate unparalleled by any other time in history. Maybe it was the jargon. The information overload. Or maybe it was just the mere fact that the mainstream media refused to give the common guy any credit. Their hollow sermons stopped short of saying, "Forget about it, you wouldn't understand." Whatever the case, no one seemed interested.

Despite his discouragement with the public's lack of awareness, he was happy to exploit it when he needed to. Although Phantom did not know it yet, he and Blake were playing a game of chess. Having his opponent's home address unquestionably extended Blake's list of possible moves. But in his experience, the best option usually required putting boots on the ground. He was no stranger to good old-fashioned espionage but given the circumstances, he thought it most effective if those boots had a higher heel.

Blake pulled his phone from his pocket, held a button, and spoke into the device. "Call Jo on speaker."

Anja picked up on the first ring.

"Jo, it's me. I'm gonna need your help."

12

"Y ou should shut it off," Anja said.

Blake turned the key and the low grumble of the Challenger's idling motor turned to silence.

Anja peered down the quiet residential street toward a small brick cape a few hundred yards away, keeping her eyes on the target.

"I hope we're right about this kid," Anja said.

"Has to be him. I'm sure of it," Blake responded.

Blake scanned the neighborhood. He noticed the similarity in the houses, the plainness of the yards. There were cars parked in drive-ways. Along the curb, minivans, worn sedans, and old SUVs. Blake wondered how many neighborhoods just like this one there were in the country. Millions. Millions of people living average lives, on unre-markable streets, toiling away in ordinary jobs for their entire lives. He wondered what it would have been like to live that kind of life. Would he have lived in this neighborhood? Gotten married and had three kids? Driven a minivan? He never would have met Anja.

Three regrets. This isn't one of them.

"Keep an eye on the house. I want to double-check something," Anja said.

Blake focused his attention on the house. Anja took out her phone and pulled up the web portal for the Accurint database. The service, often used by law enforcement, compiles records from various sources-such as utility and credit card bills -to assist investigators in identifying and locating individuals.

"Accurint shows the same thing you found. Two residents. Cathy Beck, 63, and Brandon Beck, 26. It looks like Cathy works for the town of Culpeper. There's no info on where Brandon works, if he does at all. For all we know, this Phantom could be either of them, right?" Anja said.

Blake smiled, eyes still trained on the home of Brandon Beck. "I'm gonna go out on a limb and say, between the two of them, the mom is exponentially less likely to be a closet hacktivist."

Anja did not respond. The two sat in silence for several minutes. Blake ran through the plan in his mind, trying to consider every contingency.

"Thank you for doing this. I mean, you don't have to," Anja said.

"Jo. Please. I told you. If there's anything I can do to help you. With anything. Please don't hesitate. Besides, it's fun, right? Stakeout and all."

"Oh yeah, it's a blast," she said wryly. "Honestly, it is nice to get out of the office and at least have some hope of finding a lead. This one just has not been going well and I've got everyone breathing down my neck. Most of the team is lost when it comes to the computer stuff. On top of it, I've been having to deal with Jacob Milburn, who's a complete dick. Pardon my French."

"Who's Jacob Milburn?" Blake said.

"CEO and President of IPFG," she answered. "The guy's getting all fired up about the investigation, but he's been no help. At all."

"Hopefully, we come up with something that can help. Even a little info can go a long way in getting everyone off your back," he said.

"You," Anja started. "I was going to say you haven't changed a bit, but that's really not true. There is something different about you. You seem, I don't know, more content."

"I'm definitely in a different place in my life."

"Blake," Anja said. "When I left, I mean, just because I left, doesn't mean I didn't."

"I know," Blake said, placing his hand gently on hers. "But who says there are no second chances?"

Blake saw Anja's alluring eyes begin to glisten as she reached over with her other hand and squeezed his. The moment was brief but powerful. It contained proof the connection they once shared had not died, but merely remained indefinitely suspended in time.

Anja casually pulled back her hands and discretely ran her fingers under her eyes. Her eyes widened and her body visibly tensed.

"There," she said, excitedly.

Blake turned to see a young man wearing a gray hooded sweatshirt, jeans, and a backpack emerge from the front door of the small brick house. Blake could barely make out the man's facial features from that distance.

"Brandon," Blake thought out loud.

Brandon Beck disappeared around the far side of the house and emerged with a bicycle. A BMX-style bike that looked to be two sizes too small, even for his 5'8" body.

He hopped on and began pedaling, jumped the curb at the edge of the sidewalk, and headed east on the roadway.

Blake fired up the engine and slowly pulled out, taking care to leave enough distance to not be noticed by the target.

They followed Brandon to the main road and pulled into a gas station where they had a clear view of at least another half mile of the road. The busy street was lined with strip malls and plazas. Home Depot. Best Buy. At least two different tanning salons.

About two hundred yards away, on the opposite side of the street, Blake could see Brandon leaning his bike against the side of the Starbucks and walking toward the entrance.

Perfect.

Blake pulled out, made his way across the lanes, and pulled into the Starbucks parking lot.

"Ready, Jo?" Blake asked as he pulled a Sarah J. Maas hardcover and Samsung phone from the glove compartment, handing them to her. "You clear on what you have to do?"

"Yeah, I'm good. Wish me luck," she said as she took the props, closed the car door, and walked into the shop.

Anja stepped into line just behind Brandon Beck. She could not tell from a distance but could now see that the boy had a light, wispy beard.

"Oh my god. I love the smell of this place," she said.

Beck looked over his shoulder for a moment and then returned to facing the back of a large man wearing a blue windbreaker and a Bluetooth headset.

"I don't even know what I should order," she said again, making sure Beck knew she was directing her comments toward him.

"You've never been to Starbucks?" Beck finally said.

"No. Is that weird?" she asked, trying her best to come across as quirky, if not ditzy. "I don't drink coffee that much. Usually tea. I'm supposed to meet my friend Lucy here. It was her idea. Not for, like, a while though. I thought I could just sit and read my book."

Beck turned slightly. Anja could see a thawing in his face and posture. "What you want is the chai latte." He gestured to the menu board. "See, all the way to the right there."

"Okay. Chai latte. Thanks."

Beck approached the counter, ordered, and then sat down at a small table with a chair on one side and a plush bench on the other. He pulled a laptop from his bag and set up on the table in front of him.

Anja ordered the chai latte and waited by the counter. She kept her attention on the vacant table directly next to where Brandon was seated. She figured she would keep a distance for the moment unless someone else posed a threat of taking the vacant table in the meantime.

Blake walked in, ignoring Anja as he got in line.

"Brandon," the barista called out. "Triple venti vanilla latte."

Brandon stood up from his laptop and quickly scooped his drink off the counter, all the while looking back at the open device.

"Cheri, your chai," the barista said as he handed the paper cup to Anja.

Anja casually moved to the table adjacent to Beck and sat on the bench seat that ran the length of the wall. She took a sip and said, "Oh my god. This is so delicious. You were so right."

Beck picked his head up from the screen and said with a smile, "See, I wouldn't steer you wrong." He immediately returned his focus to the screen and began furiously typing.

Anja opened her book and settled in. Blake had gotten his grande black coffee and taken a seat at a table near the front windows where he opened his own laptop and effectively blended into the scene.

After a few minutes, Anja reached into her pocket, pulled out a phone and began tapping at the screen loudly.

"Oh no, uh, my phone is dead," she said into the air. "Are there plugs in here?"

She pulled a charging cable from her pocket, moving in large enough gestures to be distracting.

"I don't have the thingy that goes into the wall. Great!" She motioned to Beck. "Hey, sorry to bother you, you're probably busy, but do you have a charger I could borrow? My phone died and I'm missing the plug thingy." She dangled the cord toward him.

"Sorry, I don't," he said, sincerely.

"Uh. I just need to check if Lucy called or texted. If I could just call her quick." She paused. "I have this cord. Do you think you could plug my phone into your computer for a few minutes to charge?"

Beck hesitated.

"Please. Just a few minutes 'til I can turn it on and check. Please. You'd be my, like, knight in shining armor," she pleaded.

"Yeah. Okay. A few minutes. I don't want to drain my battery," he relented.

"Thank you!" she squealed, handing Beck the phone and cord, then bending over and giving him a hug. "You're awesome."

Beck smiled and shook his head. "No problem," he said softly, as he plugged the cord into one of his laptop's USB ports.

Anja figured she would supply a bit of charm and a little physical contact, then let the young man's hormones do the rest of the work. She discreetly shot a look of disbelief at Blake.

Blake monitored his laptop as the device connected to Beck's computer wirelessly transmitted every bit of data on his hard drive and RAM to Blake's system. He had set up the software ahead of time to search for particular files and key words, such as "PH4N7oM," as the data was copying. He did not have time to conduct a full examination, but he wanted to at least be sure of two things: that they had the right guy and that he was using this computer for his illicit activities, especially during the time when the University of Virginia intrusion occurred. The rest, he could bluff.

Anja saw Blake close his laptop. He gave Anja a nod, suggesting he had found enough to proceed with the plan.

Anja scooted along the bench until she was just about touching Beck. Beck looked at her with puzzlement. Blake sat down on the other side of the young hacker, sliding in close.

"Brandon," Blake said as he closed the screen of Beck's laptop, "we need to talk."

"Who the hell are you?" Beck demanded.

"Who I am is not important," Blake responded. "Who she is, though? Well, that's what you should be worried about."

Beck looked at Anja with confusion.

"Agent Kohler, FBI," she said.

"Here's the thing, Mr. Phantom. That device you just plugged into your computer allowed me to copy your entire system, bit for bit, memory and all."

Anja added, "This type of scenario should be pretty concerning

86

to someone who, say, committed a dozen felonies and is facing a multitude of state and federal charges."

"Am I being arrested?" Beck asked blankly.

"That depends," Anja replied.

"What do you want? Please, I don't want to go to jail."

"Metus," Blake said, bluntly.

"Metus? What? Was it you who sent me that message? I knew it. It couldn't have been him. That's how you found me isn't it?"

"So, you know him?" Blake pressed.

"No dude-Sir. I know of him. I know only a select few have ever even spoken to him."

"How can you be sure he even exists at all?" Anja asked.

"'Cause I met a guy who saw him in person. He told me about it. Crazy story."

"Well, why don't you tell us about it?" Anja said.

"If I do, are you going to let me go?"

"We'll talk about that after we hear what you have to say," Anja said.

"Who is this friend?" Blake asked.

"Just a guy. I don't know his real name. He goes by DarkKnight. Met him at a rally in D.C. He found out I was cool with the CEA and we were smokin' up and bantering and whatnot. Then he told me he met Metus. Said the guy is psycho. Said he used to be a big shot at some bank, but I don't think that's true 'cause he said Metus looks like Freddy Kruger. Imagine Freddy Kruger working at a bank. That's messed up."

"Wait," Blake stopped him. "Freddy Kruger, you mean he's burned?"

"Yeah. But not only that. He said he was supposed to join a special group. Said it was supposed to be the best of the best, but when he got there, everyone was all burnt up just like Metus. The messed up part was they were going to burn him up too. That's what he said anyway."

"You said, 'when he got there.' When he got where?" Anja said.

"I don't know. Some church or something. Knight said a whole bunch of guys called The Disciples live together in some old church. They almost never leave. Knight said he snuck out in the middle of the night and ran before they could torch him."

"How do I get in touch with this DarkKnight?" Blake said.

"I don't know. I haven't seen him online at all in months. He's completely dark." Beck paused. "So, what's gonna happen to me?"

"You are going to go home. You are going to answer your phone if and when I call you. You will not mention this conversation to anyone. We will have you on twenty-four-hour surveillance, including all digital communication, are we clear? Here is my card. Call me if you remember anything else. We'll deal with your past activities at a later time." She stood up to allow Beck out from behind the table.

He grabbed his laptop, stuffed it in his bag, and hurried out the door. Blake could see him dodging traffic as he crossed the busy street on his bicycle.

"Well that went better than expected. Think he's telling the truth?" Anja said.

"He knew about the burns. I think whoever he was talking to was probably telling the truth, or at least some portion of it. That means you need to find yourself a church," Blake said as the two headed through the front door.

"Will you drop me off at the office?"

"Of course."

"You know, I can't use the data you stole against him. Legally, I mean," Anja said.

Blake shrugged. "I know. But it's good leverage. You might find it useful down the road."

"Good thing too, 'cause I wouldn't even know how to begin explaining to the Bureau how I got it," she laughed.

"So, Jo. Tomorrow's Friday. What do you say about having dinner with me?" Blake asked.

"Is this a business invitation or a romantic invitation?" Anja asked as Blake opened the passenger door of the car.

"Definitely romantic," Blake replied with a smile.

"In that case, it's a date."

13

"This is probably going to sting," Nine said, as he began to unwind the gauze from Thirteen's head. "Sit still."

Thirteen winced as the fabric peeled away from his oozing flesh.

Nine stopped and dropped the bundle. The long tail of gory bandages hung down into a pile on the floor. Nine reached under the antique hospital bed and turned a crank, propping up Thirteen until he was in a fully upright position.

"I don't think I can make it, Nine. It's too much," Thirteen lamented. "Please. I need painkillers. Just a little. Please," he moaned. "I think I need to go to the hospital."

"Drugs are not what you need. Narcotics, antibiotics, these are the tools of Satan. Evil's attempt to trick man into believing he can circumvent God. You must resist the temptation. You must remain pure. God will see you through."

"I'm not like you and the others. I think I'm just weak." Thirteen groaned at the stabbing pain accompanying every tug of the bandage.

"As your faith strengthens, so will your resolve," Nine preached.

"You are a soldier of God. You must not fight the pain. You must embrace it."

Thirteen tried. He had searched for days, looking inside himself to find the fortitude that Metus had promised was there. The warrior who was supposed to be released by the purification ritual. But he could find only despair. He admonished himself for being a doubter.

"There," Nine said, detaching the last bit of the wrap. He picked up a jar of greasy ointment. "This will sooth you. Help you heal."

"Wait. Let me see first," pleaded Thirteen.

Nine bowed his head and let out an annoyed sigh. "Yes." He slipped out of the room and returned with a two-foot-long piece of broken mirror.

Thirteen pinched the shard between his two tightly bandaged hands and gazed at the atrocity on the other side of the glass with detached curiosity. Second- and third-degree burns had replaced his creamy skin with a tapestry of putrid colors. Black. White. Red. Puss oozed from his raw, broken flesh. Blisters mixed with strips of charred muscle. It was a horrific injury, without question. He found no familiarity in the live portrait. No sense of connection with the reflection. He truly was no longer himself.

"It's the second degree burns that hurt. Look." Nine pressed on an area of blackened flesh. "Can you feel that?"

"Not really," Thirteen said.

"That's because the nerve endings were destroyed. The painful areas will heal soon, and scar tissue will bridge the gaps. You must give it time. Now let me apply the ointment."

Thirteen settled and allowed Nine to complete his task. The man the others sometimes called "the Deacon," when Metus was not present, oversaw rehabilitation. Much like how Two oversaw training.

Thirteen had not yet been allowed to train with the others, but he had been allowed to observe a session before his initiation. He watched as the men folded away their cots and slid their trunks to the edges of the sanctuary, creating an open space in the center of the room. There the men practiced hand-to-hand combat techniques and weapons drills. In his state, he could not imagine being able to recover enough to participate in the training. But he knew the time would come when he would be required to learn.

"Now rest," Nine said, replacing the jar on a small table sitting against the wall.

Thirteen nodded and closed his eyes. Nine turned the crank to lower the back of the bed.

Thirteen waited a few moments after he heard the rubbing of the door on the frame, then he opened his eyes, swung his feet onto the floor and shuffled to the door.

A splinter of wood embedded itself in his bare foot, the third in two days. He reached down and plucked the half-inch-long sliver of ash out of his heel. He pressed up against the door.

Moisture had swelled the ornate, ten-foot-tall door, making it impossible for it to be completely closed. He peeked through the gap, into the rectory parlor, to be sure Nine was gone.

Thirteen had spent days looking at only the four walls of his room. Walls that were completely devoid of any decoration, unless you counted the patterns of cracked plaster as a kind of abstract art. There was a stained-glass window, beautifully depicting a glowing crucifix, but it offered no view of the outside world.

He was becoming claustrophobic. With only a bed and a small table, the room began to feel more like a prison cell. But he was not to leave, not even for a moment, until his transformation was complete. Those were the express instructions Metus gave him. The isolation, he was told, was an important step in the process, and he must not have any contact with anyone, other than Nine.

The room was one of two that were part of the so-called rectory located at the back of the building, behind the elevated stage that held a pulpit and a long wooden altar.

The other room was Metus's. In comparison to the rehabilitation room, Metus's room was decadent. Artwork, plush bedding, and modern conveniences adorned the space. Thirteen was not envious, he would be more than content just being given his cot and joining the others on the sanctuary floor. But he had spent hours looking out the crack toward Metus's room, wondering what would come next, and trying to take his mind off of the excruciating pain.

There was no movement in the rectory, and no matter how hard he strained, he could not hear the conversations of the men in the sanctuary. Although he could not tell the time by the light through the stained glass, he knew it had been afternoon for some time. He guessed the others were probably in the crypt holding afternoon mass.

Thirteen dragged himself to the table that held a bedpan, urinal, and Nine's assortment of bandages and ointments. He picked up the urinal and relieved himself. It would be dinner soon, he hoped.

He sat on the bed and thought about how he wished he could sit at one of the five computer terminals that sat along the long altar in the main sanctuary. Powerful machines with blazing fast Internet connections. He smiled at the prospect. *Soon,* he told himself. *Soon I can put my talents to use.*

Thirteen's daydream was interrupted by the sound of tires crunching along the gravel driveway toward the rear of the church. Through the window, he could hear a car door closing. Had he lost that much time? Was it already time for the deliveries?

Then came the knocking at the rectory door. The squeak of the rusted hinges. The voices.

Thirteen hobbled to the door. Another splinter drove itself into the ball of his foot. He ignored it.

There were two hushed voices. One was Metus. The other he did not recognize.

He peered through the crack to see Metus shaking hands with another man. Although he could only see the back of the mysterious new visitor, he could tell the man was not a soldier. He had hair. Thick gray hair that fell against the collar of his blazer.

94

Despite the waves of pain running through his body, he willed himself to stay still and quiet. He listened to the two men speak. A tinge of shame mounted an objection to the voyeurism, but his intense boredom and need for stimulation overruled.

"The letters have been delivered. Is everything in order for phase two?" asked the unknown man, his voice soft but confident.

"Yes, and no," Metus responded. "We are in place, but an issue arose. It looks like we may not be able to gain the level of access we need by hitting the second target."

"Do you have an alternative?"

"The alternative would be to hit the L Street branch a second time, but I don't think that's a viable option. Andre Lopes lost his position, so we no longer have an inside guy. The last information we had was that security had been beefed up with armed guards and redundant bio/passcode timed locks on the physical server rooms and systems. We anticipated that all attention would be directed at securing this facility, leaving the second target vulnerable." Metus dropped his voice further. "Unfortunately, our initial analysis of the second target turned out to be flawed."

"Four days, Ray. You have four days to fix it," the gray-haired man seethed.

"I'm well aware of the timeline, and the stakes."

"There's another thing," the man said. "The man I was telling you about, Blake Brier. He's been putting pieces together and building a narrative for himself. If you let him continue as he is, he will pose a major threat. I made contact, set it in motion. You've waited too long. Do you get what I'm saying?"

"I will take care of it," Metus promised.

The man paused. "How is your new recruit coming along?"

Metus motioned to the door of the rehabilitation room. Thirteen's heart rate increased.

"Fine," he whispered, "but he's months out from being any use to me. The bigger problem is, if this fails, or even if it doesn't, all hell is going to break loose. I'm going to need loyal soldiers. Many more of them."

"You're the one who insists on playing Jesus," the man snarled. "Look, I'm impressed with what you've done here. But I think you know it's not sustainable. It's too complicated."

"There's a bigger picture to think about. I'm building a movement that goes well beyond the mission at hand. You don't understand because you have no faith. I give these men purpose. I give them a path to salvation. Just as God saved me, he will save their souls. Our cause is righteous, it is his will. Besides, indoctrination is an art. Genius or not, I challenge you to get anyone to commit to a suicidal mission without hesitation."

"Fair enough, but can you at least refrain from killing innocent people. The tellers? What the hell was that? Fear is a useful tool, but you can't alienate the masses if you want your message to resonate on a larger scale."

"It is a crusade. It's time that blood was shed. And you must admit, it was beautiful. You really must watch the video that Lopes sent over. It was like a ballet. My men trained for months to synchronize the executions at that exact time. It's a shame no one seemed to get the message, the reference to the scripture passage. The FBI, the media. They are sheep. They have no imagination."

"You are a sick man, Ray. That wasn't part of the plan. You killed those people because you get some sick pleasure out of it. No other reason. The same pleasure you get out of burning these poor kids. Your depravity is mind boggling."

Metus shrugged. "I am but a vessel, remember? I get my orders from God himself."

Thirteen shuddered at the statement. Not at the words themselves, but at the way they were said. A flippant, smug proclamation that, in an instant, put everything in perfect perspective.

He's a fraud! The thought churned Thirteen's stomach. The pain radiating throughout his body amplified. He hurried toward the table and heaved over the steel bedpan.

He slid onto the bed and forced himself to lie still. His heart raced and his thoughts swirled. As the sound of the car door and crunching gravel receded, Thirteen, Aaron, was absorbed by the realization that he was in extreme peril.

He resolved to devote everything, his entire being, to finding an answer to one all-consuming question: *What do I do now?*

14

"Here you are, Mr. Milburn." Sheryl handed him a piping hot cup of Starbucks coffee from across the street. Every morning, it was the same routine. Deliver the coffee, run through the appointments, and get any documents signed that she prepared after Milburn left the day before.

"And?" Milburn glanced at his watch. Twice.

"You have a teleconference at ten with Fidelity, lunch with Omnicom at noon about the TV spots, and the afternoon is clear, just like you asked. Also, don't forget you have dinner tomorrow evening. Oh, and your son's waiting in the lobby. Again."

"Get rid of him," Milburn said. "Or let him sit there, I don't care. He can come every day if it suits him but if he thinks he's going to get any money out of me he'll be waiting a long time. What else?"

"I do have these for you to sign, but there's something else." Sheryl produced several pieces of paper and a ripped envelope. "It's a letter from the CEA. I was going to call the FBI, but I wanted to show it to you first."

"Give it to me." Milburn snatched the letter. "I'll take care of this with the FBI. Any communication about the investigation will go through me, period. Do you understand?"

"Yes, sir."

"Now leave me."

Sheryl was almost out the door when Milburn called after her.

"And Sheryl?"

"Yes?"

"Get rid of him."

"I will."

Milburn read through the letter, word by word. His temperature rose and, within seconds, perspiration began shimmering on his reddening skin.

He dropped the letter, opened his desk drawer, and pulled out an old flip phone. He powered it on and dialed.

"We need to talk. In person. Will you put it together? As many as can make it, you set the time. Just make it before Monday. Let me know." He hung up and returned the phone to his desk drawer.

He got up and walked to a small glass table, stocked with several brands of bourbon and Scotch. He poured three fingers into a glass and drank it down with complete disregard for the fact that it was eight o'clock in the morning.

For a few minutes, he paced a circular route around his desk. Finally, he sat and made several calls, one after the other. When he finished, he pressed the intercom button. "Sheryl, can you come in here?"

"Yes, Mr. Milburn?" she said, appearing ten seconds later.

"Sheryl, I feel like I haven't told you what a good job you've been doing. I have a surprise for you."

15

The crystal goblets rang out as Blake and Anja gently tapped them together.

"To a night off," Blake said.

"To new beginnings," Anja added.

The two sipped the rich Merlot. Blake savored its complex flavor.

Piano music filled the room, a hair louder than the sum of the muted conversations taking place around the dining room. The pianist, positioned on a raised platform at the other end of the room, played softly and delicately. The dim light, dark velvety colors, and large plush chairs and booths had a soothing effect. Blake was pleased by his choice of location.

"So, did you find the church?" he asked.

"Not yet. We have several people going through land records and checking out addresses. The reactions from the priests and pastors have not been particularly warm, as you can imagine. 'Hello, do you happen to have a band of sadistic monsters living here by any chance?' Doesn't go over well."

"I bet. But maybe you're looking at this the wrong way. Maybe you should be looking for a defunct or abandoned church. A temple or hall, or something. Or even a place that's just reminiscent of a church. I figure it would have to be remote, right? Otherwise the neighbors would certainly notice something was up," Blake suggested.

"We're looking at all kinds of options, but it's going to take some time. It was hard enough convincing Wells to chase this lead. I told him and Harrison that the info came from one of my more reliable informants. It's a miracle Wells never asked who."

"You'll put it all together, I know you will. It's just a matter of time."

"I know, but I'm running out of time." Anja threw her hands up in an exasperated gesture. "That's the other thing. I didn't get a chance to tell you. We got a letter. A kind of warning. Something else is coming, Blake. Something worse. I have to find these guys. Stop them before more people get hurt."

"A letter? What did it say?"

"A bunch of cryptic junk. Scriptures, mostly. A bunch of hyperbole, you know, doomsday stuff. I can't remember the exact words, but I'll let you read it later. The important thing is that it refers to an event, like an attack. Of course, it doesn't say what or when or where. Seeing the aftermath in the bank, what they're capable of, I can't even imagine."

Anja stopped, took another sip of wine, and flashed Blake a wide smile.

"But that's work," she said, "this night is about you and me." She leaned close, bringing her glass to his once more.

"To good company," he said, compelled to assign the extra clink its own tagline.

"So, fill me in. You work from home writing computer code full time now, right? What made you leave Booz? God, you used to be so dedicated to that job," she said.

There's the accent again.

"Jo, that's what I've been wanting to talk to you about. There are some things you don't know. Some things I've always wished I could tell you but, honestly, I never thought I would actually get the opportunity. You know, things get complicated. Not that you, we, were complicated. It's just that, you know, other things."

"What is it, Blake? Just tell me. It's water under the bridge now, right? Were you having an affair?"

"An affair? No. Hell no! Far from it. The thing is, I never actually worked for Booz Allen."

"What do you mean? You worked there for years," she said. Her eyes began to squint.

"I'm sorry, Jo. When we met, Booz Allen Hamilton was my official cover for being stationed in Stuttgart. I worked for the Agency, Jo."

"The Agency? The CIA? Wait, what?"

"Please, understand Jo. I know I shouldn't have let you get mixed up with me. At first, I told myself it would work. That I could maintain the lie. It got harder and harder the more I had to travel. I wanted to tell you, I just couldn't. If you knew the truth, it could have compromised the entire team."

"The team? What did you do for them? Were you a coder? An analyst?"

"Spec Ops," he said.

"Spec Ops? This makes so much more sense now."

"What does?" he asked.

"Everything. I mean the way you were, the things you seemed to know about, the secrecy. God, I would have sworn you were cheating," Anja said.

"Jo. I never did. I never would. Look, it's all out there now, so I'll just tell you. I love you, Jo. I always have. It was the hardest thing I have ever done in my life. To watch you leave and not try to stop you."

"I left because it didn't seem like you wanted me anymore. Like you'd be better off without me."

"I know. The deeper I got, the more missions I completed, the more I realized I was putting you in danger. You were an obvious leverage point, a way to get at me. I couldn't keep you in that position, but I couldn't bring myself to break it off. It was tearing me up. I know I became distant. I know I was standoffish. But when you suggested leaving, I also knew the right thing to do was to let you go."

Anja took Blake's hand, leaned close, and pressed her lips against his. Her kiss was soft and tentative yet charged with underlying passion. Blake felt as if electricity had surged through his body, the feeling of having the power to right a profound wrong. To turn back time.

She pressed her forehead against his.

"So, you're a certified badass then," she joked, placing her hand on his chest.

"*Was* a certified badass," he said. "Now I'm just an average guy, trying as hard as I can to live an average, boring life."

"And how's that going for you?"

"Well, I've got the boring part down pat," he said.

"Maybe we need to spice it up a bit."

"Okay, I like the sound of that. What'd you have in mind?"

"Let's get out of here," she whispered.

Blake could feel the energy building around them. He knew she could too. "You sure? We haven't even ordered yet," he said. A sly smile crept onto his face.

"Are you *that* hungry?" She slid her hand onto the inner part of his thigh.

Blake's hand sprang upward in a telegraphing gesture and, as if gratified by being able to use the TV trope in a real-life context, he hollered: "Waiter, check please."

16

Blake traced his fingertips along the silky arm that was lightly draped across his chest. Soft, ethereal breath against his neck sent a prickling sensation through his scalp. He ran his other hand down the small of Anja's back and pressed her tightly to him, the warmth of her bare skin combining with his. Blake sensed her fragility, a striking contrast to the strength and tenacity which normally defined her. An overwhelming urge came over him. A need to protect her, to keep her safe.

The light from a single candle flickered off the ceiling and gave a fiery shimmer to the white satin sheets that sparsely covered their entangled bodies. Blake felt an extraordinary sense of clarity, fueled by a mixture of euphoria and exhaustion. He noticed the black and white Ansel Adams photographs framed and evenly spaced along the walls of Anja's bedroom. The orange strobe reflected off the images of trees, mountains, and giant monoliths. A reminder of the possibilities. The opportunities and experiences that would be possible in his new life. An alternate future. One he hoped would include Anja.

"What are you thinking?" Anja whispered, her groggy voice sweet and vulnerable.

"I thought you were sleeping," Blake said. "I was just thinking you're a talented interior decorator. Maybe you can lend your skills to my place, God knows I need it."

Anja chuckled.

"Sorry to disappoint but I can't take credit for any of it. Cole Prévost. They did the whole place. If I didn't hire someone, I'd probably still be living out of cardboard boxes."

"Well, it suits you," he said.

Anja lifted her head and propped herself up on her elbow. She leaned over and pressed her lips against his.

"Do you think we could just stay right here forever?" Anja asked.

"We could certainly try. I'm willing to give it a shot."

Anja rested her head in her hand. Blake reached out, touched her cheek with his thumb, and pushed a hanging lock of blonde hair behind her ear.

"What were *you* thinking about?" he asked.

"A lot of things," she said. "You, mostly. This. Us. And a guy named Reid."

"Wow, I guess I missed the mark," Blake said, jokingly.

Anja let out a laugh.

"Let me assure you Mr. Brier, you delivered a stellar performance," Anja said, running her fingernails playfully over the contour of Blake's abdominal muscles.

"What I mean is, I feel bad for him. He was an IT guy at the bank. I asked him to help me out, to see if he could tell what the suspects were looking for on the company's computer system. When Milburn found out, he fired Reid on the spot. I guess I can't help but feel responsible."

"That's not on you," Blake consoled. "You couldn't have known. It makes no sense to begin with. You weren't kidding, this Milburn really does sound like a douche."

"A lot of things don't make any sense about this whole thing," she said, sliding her hand beneath the sheet at Blake's waist. "I've got an idea of what will take my mind off it."

Blake's body responded. He could feel the rush of blood flowing toward her touch.

"Mmmm. Hold that thought," she said, teasingly, as she pulled back her hand and rolled out of bed. "I'll be right back."

Anja slid toward the bathroom and flicked on the light. She turned back and smiled at Blake. The flood of light through the doorway accentuated her curves and slim muscular build. Blake absorbed the stunning beauty of her nude form as if he were contemplating a rare masterpiece hanging on the wall of the National Gallery. Anja closed the door, sending the room back into the pulsing orange glow.

Blake pushed himself up and leaned his back against the sturdy wooden headboard. He heard a faint sound, like that of movement. He wondered if he was hearing things. Blake sat up straight and listened closely. He heard the unmistakably sharp sound of glass shattering somewhere in the apartment, outside the bedroom.

"Are you okay, Jo?" he called out.

"Yeah, I'll just be a minute," she answered through the door.

Blake stepped out of bed and slid his jeans on. He walked to the door, straining to listen to any subtle noises. He glanced at the small marble table beside the bed where Anja's service weapon was resting in its holster. He decided against taking it with him.

Blake slowly turned the knob and opened the door a crack.

Smash. The door swung open, striking Blake in the temple. Blake instinctively dropped to one knee.

The muzzle of an automatic pistol entered the room first, followed by the outstretched arms of a tall, muscular figure, clad in all black.

Before the intruder could register that Blake was directly beneath him, Blake thrust himself upward, out of his crouched position, and struck the underside of his attacker's forearm with the palm of his left hand. Simultaneously, Blake delivered a hammer fist blow to the man's wrist, snapping both the radius and ulna between the two leverage points. The sickening sound of bones splintering was drowned out by the discharge of the silver firearm. The impact had caused a sympathetic trigger pull, sending a single round into the wall, well clear of Blake's head.

Blake followed through in a circular motion, folding the attacker's hand toward his body. The sharp ends of the two bones tore through the flesh of the forearm. The pistol dropped from the limp hand as the attacker screamed in agony.

Blake spun toward the figure, driving his fist into the man's solar plexus. As he did so, he found himself face to face with his attacker. Only, it was not a face that looked back at him, but a smooth white mask.

CEA.

Blake leaned his weight into a punch that landed just under the masked man's jaw line, above his Adam's apple. Blake clawed upward at the mask, pushing up and over the man's head, revealing the horrifically scarred flesh that hid beneath. His bloodshot eyes bulged as he grasped at his throat and fell to his knees, unable to emit a sound.

As the writhing man collapsed, Blake could see another masked figure moving toward him from the pitch-dark hallway. The flickering candlelight barely escaped the bedroom and reflected back off of the bright white mask, betraying the second attacker's position. Dressed in black from head to toe, the mask appeared to be hovering in midair, slowly drifting toward the doorway. Blake balled his fists and bent his knees slightly, preparing for combat.

It took a moment for Blake to process that the second attacker was armed with a black semi-automatic handgun, which, he came to realize, was pointed at his chest. The matte black weapon blended in with the black clothing, but Blake could see by the contrast of the trigger guard that the man's pasty white index finger was pressed against the trigger.

Blake instantaneously weighed all his options and came to the conclusion that it would not be possible to cover the distance between himself and the gunman before he was able to fire at least once. He decided to buy himself time.

"Stay back," the masked man said. The timbre of his voice had an ordinary quality, much younger sounding then Blake would have imagined.

Blake raised his hands and slowly moved backward and to the right, attempting to block the man's view of Anja's pistol, laying out in the open a few feet behind him.

"Blake Brier?" the man asked.

How does this crazy person know my name?

"Who's asking?" Blake replied.

"Who else lives here?" the man asked.

"Just me," Blake said. "Let's relax, okay? Just tell me what you want. I'm not going to give you any trouble. There's two of you and one of me, right? Wouldn't make sense for me to resist."

The man turned his head toward his accomplice, still crumpled on the floor in pain, gasping for breath. His pale face now darkened to a purple hue.

"Turn around and kneel down," the gunman said, releasing his left hand from the gun and pulling a roll of duct tape from the front pocket of his hooded sweatshirt.

Blake slowly spun around, trying to further shorten the distance between him and the bedside table. He knelt facing the black handle protruding from the holster, four feet in front of him.

Still too far.

Blake could not be sure the masked man hadn't already seen the weapon. He figured the only viable play would be to cooperate. To hunker down for the long haul.

Blake was grateful Anja had remained quietly hidden in the bathroom. The last thing he wanted to do was startle the man with his finger precariously wrapped around the trigger of a gun. A gun that was relentlessly pointed at any number of his vital organs.

Blake thought it lucky that Anja had recently learned the truth about his past. If she didn't believe he could take care of himself, she was apt to do something impulsive trying to save him. On the other hand, Blake thought, if Anja had not been completely naked and unarmed, or had some means of communication with the outside world, the situation might have been significantly easier to manage.

"Keep your hands raised," the man directed. "If you move, I will shoot you."

The man bolstered the verbal threat by pressing the muzzle into the back of Blake's head. Blake felt the cold steel against his scalp. He could feel the adrenaline surge through his body. Not triggered by fear, but excitement. The man had made a critical mistake. He had given up his only advantage. Distance.

Blake pivoted on one knee, pushing his body to the side as he grasped the gun with both hands. He violently twisted the pistol, easily freeing it from the gunman's hand. Before the lapse of another second, Blake sent a round through the thin plastic mask and into the brain of his attacker. The man flopped to the floor, motionless. Blake pulled the mask from his face. His hideous deformation made him appear to be an exact replica of his accomplice.

Blake turned his attention to the first man, who had started rising to his knees. His skin bright red and swollen. The silver handgun rested on the floor, within an arm's length.

"Don't," Blake warned.

The man remained silent, only emitting a labored wheezing sound. But his body language was loud and unequivocal. He was making his last stand. There was no question in Blake's mind, he was going to try to reach the gun.

Blake calmly trained the sights of the borrowed pistol on the man's head and then moved the sight picture to about a foot to the left, an approximation of where the man's head would be if he were to lean over to grasp his weapon with his left hand.

The wheezing abruptly stopped. He saw the man's shoulders dip. Calm and prepared, Blake thought the man might as well have been moving in slow motion. He smoothly pressed the trigger. The bullet entered the man's skull, just above the ear, before his outstretched fingertips could touch the handle of the gun.

Blake moved to the door of the bedroom, reached around, and

flicked the hallway light switch. Gun raised, he scanned the hallway and listened for any further movement. Finding no immediate threat, he moved backward into the bedroom, closed the door, and locked it.

"Jo. You can come out. Get dressed, I've still gotta clear the rest of the place. You're going to have to call your people in," he said, as he checked the pockets of the two deceased combatants.

There was no answer.

"Jo?" he said again, moving toward the bathroom door.

Still no answer.

Blake opened the door and moved into the bathroom. "Come on Jo, we've gotta move."

"Jo. No! No!" Blake darted toward Anja, slipping through a pool of blood that had expanded from under her lifeless body. He dropped to his knees, wrapped his arms under her, and lifted her upper body toward him. Her head fell back, weighing heavily on her delicate neck. He could see a small bullet hole just below her right breast.

He hoisted her toward him until her torso was fully upright. He checked her back and saw a large exit wound, a few inches wide. "Please, Jo. No! Stay with me," he cried.

Blake had seen his share of trauma in the field and understood the injuries Anja had sustained were not survivable. But he could not believe it. He did not want to believe it. He frantically checked for a pulse but could not find the faintest sign of life.

Blake gently touched her cheek with the back of his fingers. Tears streamed down his face. His mind was tied in knots. He struggled to form a rational thought.

"Not you, Jo. Please no. Anyone else. Me, take me. I love you. You need to know that. Please know that. I'm sorry. I'm so sorry," he rambled through guttural sobs.

Blake cradled Anja's neck and pulled her head toward his chest, squeezing her tightly. Overwhelming grief exploded from the core of his soul and escaped through his lungs in an inhuman scream.

He held her for several minutes, slowly rocking. Covered in the blood of the person he cherished above all else, he fought to ball up his profound rage and push it deep into his gut.

As the minutes ticked by, Blake began to regain a sense of his surroundings. He glanced over his shoulder to see the small hole punched through the Sheetrock wall of the bathroom. Fire burned in his eyes. He brought his cheek to hers and whispered in her ear. "I swear to you. I will hunt down every last one of them, and I will kill them all. They will pay in blood. I swear it."

Blake tenderly laid Anja down and kissed her on her forehead. He looked at her face longingly. Even in death, her beauty was breathtaking. His body wanted to heave and vomit and sob some more, but his heart hardened, his eyes deadened, and he stood up from the floor with a numb resolve.

The range of emotions coursing through him were debilitating and his mind was clouded with guilt, regret, and utter sadness.

But one thing was crystal clear to him at that moment. The idea that he could ever live a normal, quiet life revealed itself as an unattainable. A pure fantasy. A futile pursuit that died right there on the bathroom floor, with Anja Kohler.

17

The water streamed down Blake's face, funneling off his beard and creating a white porcelain gap in the red puddle around his feet. Blake stood as still as a corpse. Eyes closed. Inches from the shower head.

He could hardly remember how he got from Anja's bathroom to his own. He knew he drove his car, but his recollection of the trip was obscured by a fog. Like trying to remember a dream, the harder one tries to recount the events, the more the details slip back into the unreachable parts of the mind.

Had he made the anonymous call to 911? Had he been able to erase all traces of himself from the scene while consumed by grief and rage?

Rage did not manifest itself in Blake in the same way it would in most. He did not become frantic, disorganized, impulsive. Just the opposite. Blake became cold. Calculating. Determined. Rage replaced all other innate drives. It took residence in the parts of the brain that crave food and water and burrowed down into the pit of his stomach.

He told himself he had no choice but to leave. To abandon her fragile lifeless body. It seemed cold. Irreverent. But he could not do what he needed to do under the scrutiny of an FBI investigation. Hours of questioning in FBI custody would waste precious time. That did not mean he didn't feel guilty. He tried to offset the guilt by promising himself that he would make it right once it was over. He meant it, but it did not help.

Blake was never one to feel sorry for himself. But there, with the water washing away the last physical connection he would ever have to Anja, he allowed himself to feel the sadness. For forty-five minutes he allowed it to grow, until it approached despair. And then, he let it go. Temporarily.

Time to go to work.

Blake washed, dried, and moved to the bedroom to get dressed. He put on a pair of jeans and a black T-shirt. He laced up a pair of Danner boots and bounded down the stairs.

Clunk. The actuators slid back into the thick metal door as Blake typed in the last digit of the code. He pushed the door, releasing the suction.

Blake opened the small closet, several feet behind his desk chair. Several computer components and other miscellaneous items adorned eight shallow shelves, each about eighteen inches deep. He reached for the top shelf and pulled down one of several black bags. He grasped the nylon webbing handles and held out the bag to gauge its size.

Satisfied with the random choice, he turned and slid his finger into the opening where the door latched. There was an audible clicking sound as Blake toggled a small metal tab at the back of the opening.

Blake closed the closet door, turned the handle, and immediately opened it again. This time the entire frame and closet shelves swung open on a larger, hidden frame. Blake pushed the door all the way against the wall and walked through the opening.

The thirty-by-thirty–foot room was noticeably cooler than the office. Metal shelves spanned one entire wall, stocked to capacity with canned goods, water, and other nonperishable items. A sink, toilet, and shower sat on the far wall, next to a large cot that was tucked into the corner. On the opposite wall from the food pantry were two identical standing safes, several racks of clothing, and a narrow mirror. A single horseshoe hung over the door, the only decorative item in the room.

Blake spun the dial on the rightmost safe, fluently entering the combination. He yanked on the five-foot-tall door. Dozens of firearms and hundreds of rounds of ammunition were neatly organized in customized compartments. Blake loaded twenty boxes of 9mm ammunition into the black nylon bag and left it on the floor in front of the open safe.

He moved to the clothing racks and lifted the wooden hanger which held a black leather jacket. Blake brought the arm of the jacket to his nose and sharply inhaled the distinct smell of the hide. He had worn this jacket before. Many times. The smell reminded him of the past. A past in which he did not have the luxury of reflection. But it was not a nostalgic significance that drew him to the article of clothing, as much as the functionality. The slim-fitted garment was custom made to comfortably conceal a 9mm pistol outfitted with a suppressor and allowed for incredibly quick access. Blake slid his arms into the jacket and adjusted the collar in the mirror. He caught his own eye for a moment, as though he was staring into the eyes of an old acquaintance.

Welcome back.

Blake walked to the safe and plucked a Glock 19 9mm from its holder. He slid back the slide and let it ride forward, sending a round from the magazine into the chamber. He released the magazine, grabbed a loose 9mm shell from the tray inside the safe, and returned the magazine to full capacity. All the firearms were stored with a loaded magazine but did not have a round in the chamber so the tension could be taken off the springs during long periods of storage. Unlike the one next to his bed. That one was always fully locked and loaded.

He selected a five-inch-long suppressor and screwed the cylinder onto the threaded barrel of the Glock. He slid the weapon into the inner left panel of the jacket and withdrew his empty hand in one fluid motion. He reached in and retrieved the pistol with the same smooth movement, repeating the process several more times until he was comfortable that his muscle memory hadn't faded.

Blake selected another Glock 9mm handgun and a H&K MP5 9mm submachine gun to load into the bag. With the urgency of a Walmart shopper on Black Friday, he loaded the bag with a few additional supplies. Extra magazines, flex cuffs, night-vision goggles.

He shut the safe, grabbed the bag, and moved back into the office, shutting off the light and shutting the false-closet door behind him.

Blake dropped the bag beside his chair and sat down. He took his cell phone from his pocket and dialed. A number he had committed to memory many years ago but had not dialed in some time.

"Fezz," Blake said, as the other end of the line came to life, "it's me. Are you in country?"

"Sure am. How the hell are ya? It's been a while, brotha," Fezz replied.

"I need to see you. Both of you. Can you be at Bravo in thirty minutes?" Blake questioned.

Blake was confident Fezz already understood the potential gravity of his call. When he left, he and his former team members chose five specific locations in the D.C. area that could be referred to by letter designation. Alpha, Bravo, Charlie, Delta, and Echo. In the event an issue arose, the men would be able to set a meet without disclosing the location to eavesdroppers.

The mere fact that Blake had invoked this contingency was enough to convey the seriousness of his situation. It also meant his team would take precautions to avoid being followed and would come equipped to handle any threat that might arise.

"Roger. Thirty minutes," Fezz said.

The phone disconnected.

18

Blake sped north on George Washington Memorial Parkway. His left hand pinned a small scrap of paper to the steering wheel. He strained to read his own writing in the light of the passing streetlamps: Bravo. 38.790632, -77.039707. With his right hand, he thumbed the digits into his phone's mapping app. He knew where he was going but planned to take the path less traveled.

The tires squealed as he rounded the turn onto Green Street. He headed south and followed Jones Point Drive to the end. The dark lot showed no signs of activity.

Blake wasted little time on parking and moved away from the car on foot. Moving quickly and deliberately, he took a position under the beltway where he could observe the length of Jones Point Drive. If he were followed, it wouldn't be long before he saw headlights. He checked his watch, fifteen minutes until the rendezvous. Blake stood still.

After five minutes, he began moving south into a wooded area. Avoiding a path that looped around toward the meeting point, he instead made a beeline through the trees. He pulled out his phone and headed in the direction of the red map marker, expertly traversing obstacles despite the darkness.

An acute sound, like that of dried twigs snapping, stopped Blake in his tracks. He crouched down at the base of a hackberry tree and listened. Although he had not noticed before, he could hear a symphony of background noise. The rumble of jet engines disturbing the atmosphere, the whir of trucks and cars barreling down the beltway, the nondescript industrial sounds of the city.

Then, much closer, another snap cut through the wet blanket of noise pollution. The sound of movement came closer, close enough for Blake to estimate the general direction of its source. He slid the Glock from his jacket and held it at the low-ready. He waited, silent, still.

The sound of careful, slow footsteps continued to approach. And then, stopped. Blake lifted his pistol and held it high to the side of his face. He peeked around the trunk and caught a glint of light. Two dots, separating themselves from the shadowy backdrop. He withdrew behind the cover and visualized the position of the enemy. Crouching. Prone. The eyes could not have been more than a few feet off the ground.

Blake sprung out and leveled his pistol toward the ground ten feet in front of him. His finger slid into the trigger guard and he instinctively applied enough pressure to the trigger to take out the slack. His target instantly came into focus. The calm, inquisitive face of a mangy old dog stared back at him. Blake scanned the area and lowered his gun.

The dog tilted his head as if to say, "What the hell was that about?" Blake stomped his foot and barked a muted "GITTT." The dog hopped back, startled, then stopped and resumed his defiant stare. After a moment, his head turned as if he had lost interest, and the pathetic animal sauntered off into the night.

Blake tucked the gun into his jacket, shook his head, and set out to traverse the remaining distance. He emerged from the wood line and scanned the area. His eyes were adjusted to the dark under the canopy of trees. The city lights bouncing off the overcast sky and shimmering in the Potomac provided more than adequate visibility. He glanced at his phone. The blue dot was overlapping the red waypoint.

Bravo.

To the west, about a hundred yards away, he saw two figures moving toward him on the path. Bobbing up and down in a swift jog. At a distance, the pair were reminiscent of a ringmaster leading a circus bear. From his vantage point, the larger of the two men appeared as tall as the lighthouse another hundred yards behind them. Blake felt a sense of relief. Even their silhouettes were unmistakable.

Blake stepped out into the center of the path. It took about a minute before the three men converged. They greeted each other with handshakes and hearty pats on the back.

"I try to get a few miles in every morning, but this is a little early, even for me," said Khat, a wide smile on his face.

"We ran a Spartan last month and I beat the pants off him." Fezz shoved Khat playfully. "Now he's on this running kick. I told him he's wasting his time. I'd never give him the satisfaction of beating me."

"We'll see. You're going to feel like a jerk when I smoke you," Khat taunted.

Normally, Blake would not miss an opportunity to throw in a jibe or two of his own, but he stayed quiet. Distant.

The smile left Fezz's face. "What's up Mick, are you okay? What'd you get yourself into now?"

"Look guys, sorry to pull you out here at this hour, but I need your help. There's something I need to take care of, off book. Way off book," Blake said. He anxiously stroked back his hair with both hands.

"We're listening." Khat perked up.

"Jo's dead," Blake said bluntly. He felt the lump in his throat swell. Saying it out loud made it seem more real. More final.

"Oh, Mick. I'm so sorry, brotha," Fezz said, placing his giant hand on Blake's shoulder.

The lively banter had instantly been replaced by an anxious silence.

"I don't believe it," Khat said. "How?"

"She was murdered. Murdered by sadistic maniacs." Blake's voice rose. He forced himself to drop back to a hushed tone. "Have you seen the coverage on that bank robbery, the whole thing with the hacktivist group, terrorist group, the CEA? She was investigating that case and those sick bastards came for her. I was there, Fezz. In her bedroom. I was right there and I couldn't save her."

Blake struggled not to break down. It was not that he was afraid to show his emotions. The three had suffered gut-wrenching losses together and were always a source of support for one another. But now was not the time to let his emotions run loose.

"He investigated the sky as if some better explanation was floating amongst the low hanging clouds.

Fezz and Khat had never met Anja in person but the pair had been bombarded with stories over the years. It would have been impossible for either of them to underestimate the grief Blake was experiencing. But they were hard men. Practical men. And they were exactly what Blake needed.

"Wait, back up," Fezz said. "You two got back together?"

Blake opened his mouth to answer but realized he did not know how. Were they back together? It was complicated. Instead, Blake briefed his two former teammates on the circumstances of Anja's death. Their reconnection, the home invasion, the faceless masked men.

"Sounds like you already took out the bastards," Khat interjected.

"The two were part of a larger group, led by a guy who goes by the name of Metus. You can be sure these two heathens didn't just show up on their own accord." Blake spat.

"Metus, like the Roman god?" Khat said.

"Shut up with your corny Greek mythology already," Fezz said.

"Roman. *Ro-man* mythology. Metus is the equivalent of the Greek god Deimos. The personification of terror. What kind of warrior doesn't know that?"

Fezz ignored the dig. "This dude Metus sounds like an arrogant prick if you ask me. God of terror, my butt!"

"All I know is, he's supposedly holed up in some church. That's the main reason I called: I need your help finding him. Can you pull the satellites? Without setting off the whistles?" Blake asked.

"Shouldn't be a problem," said Khat, confidently.

Blake was familiar with the capabilities of the Agency's covert spy satellite network; its product having been the basis for several of his team's missions. Codenamed "Logos," the trillion-dollar project had significantly increased the reach of the United States government over the past decade, and had become an indispensable tool for the military, CIA, NSA, and other clandestine groups. Combined, the matrix of satellites carried hundreds of thousands of advanced digital imaging sensors and precision optics, digitally stitched together to provide almost complete visual coverage of the entire globe.

Every second of the high definition video was stored indefinitely. The system leveraged artificial intelligence and computer vision to analyze imagery on the fly. Specialized software, acquired from the Israeli government, allowed autonomous culling of relevant data by visual characteristics, measurements, and predictive patterns, and could reconstruct three dimensional, three-hundred-sixty-degree video when needed. With the help of a virtual reality headset, an analyst could put themselves anywhere on earth, at any moment. And, most importantly, because there was no longer a need to redirect satellites, the information was available to anyone with access and clearance, simultaneously. While there was a need-based access request process, it had become so commonplace that it devolved to no more than a formality.

"When we find him, we're coming with you." Fezz insisted.

"I can't ask you to do that." Blake said.

"You didn't ask." Fezz replied.

"Both of our asses would be feeding the jackals back in Afghanistan if it were not for you, Mick. Consider it a chance to return the favor." Khat said.

"Here. Take this." Blake took a folded piece of paper from his jacket pocket and handed it to Khat. "This is all the info I've been able to gather. That *we* were able to gather."

Khat unfolded the document, looked it over, and stowed it away.

Blake took a hard look at the two men. "It's good to see you guys."

"It's good to see you too, brother. Go home and get some sleep," Fezz urged. "We'll let you know what we find."

"Okay. Thank you," Blake said as he backed away and quietly slipped into the woods.

The predawn sky had just begun to brighten. Blake knew sleep would not come easy, but he was revitalized by the prospect of, if he was honest, exacting revenge. Of seeing it through for Anja.

He had a mission. As clear as any he had ever been given. But for the first time, the mission was personal.

19

Andrew Harrison rolled out of bed and stumbled to the window. He pushed up the heavy shade to allow the bright morning sun to signal his body that it was time to fully wake up. He gazed out the window at the rolling farmland, adjacent to his property, Yoder Farm.

His own house had once been owned by the Yoder family, but two decades earlier they subdivided several parcels of land and sold the house to subsidize the business. The faded nineteen-thirties cape and the three acres on which it sat was bought by a family whose patriarch, about five years prior, moved the family to Switzerland for a business opportunity. Harrison became the beneficiary of a highly motivated seller. The house was old, and a bit of a money pit, but it had character. And a view. A true country setting.

The setting was the primary reason Harrison stayed in Unionville after his divorce. He certainly could do without the two-hour drive to work, especially on last minute call-ins, but it was the drive home that made it worthwhile.

As the city disappeared behind him, the multi-lane highways turned into two-lane trails, and the sky darkened to reveal the stars hidden behind the smog and the veil of light emitted by the urban sprawl, the stress of the job drained away. Not completely, but enough. Enough that Harrison could still appreciate it.

The only reason he bought the house was to give his kids a wholesome small-town upbringing. It did not exactly go according to plan, but the idea was solid. Julie hated it from day one. She had finished her degree, obtained a teaching certificate, and completed her first interview with the Boston public school system when Harrison received the transfer order.

At the time, it seemed like the perfect excuse to get away from city life. They had to buy a house somewhere near D.C., why not Unionville? There were, of course, no teaching jobs open in the surrounding counties and one was unlikely to open up. And even if there were, it would not have been the type of troubled, inner-city mentoring experience Julie envisioned.

Andy settled quickly into his eighth-grade class and transitioned easily to high school in Orange. A born athlete, he played football and baseball. In contrast, Alice did not have as easy a time. Just a year younger than Andy, Alice's interests were not well-aligned with most of the student body. She was angry that she was forced to leave the Boston ballet school, which she had attended for seven years. She did not make a single friend and slowly started to become withdrawn, even at home. She spent hours alone reading, writing, or drawing.

None of these were the reason it fell apart. Harrison could not say the exact reason. Only that, one day, he came home, and it was different. He could sense it, but all efforts to steer it back on course proved futile. It was not long before Julie announced she was taking the children back to Boston. There had been fighting. Long arguments. But in the end, it was the right thing for their kids.

He would have followed, returned to the Boston office to be closer to them. But that was not an option. Not after everything that happened. It still weighed on him. But the mandatory transfer, even the thirty-day suspension, were gifts. He had no illusions. If he had not grown up with the Congressman, if there was no one to intervene, he'd probably be driving a truck or humping shingles up a ladder every day.

On Saturday morning, usually around ten o'clock, Harrison would set aside an hour or so to video chat with Andy and Alice. It had grown into a tradition that all three of them looked forward to. Harrison was grateful to be able to maintain a great relationship with his children in the few years that had passed. He was looking forward to taking a trip up to Boston for Andy's high school graduation next month.

Harrison set the alarm on his phone for ten o'clock. He planned to put a few hours in, tinkering in the detached garage, and did not want to lose track of time.

Too small to fit his car, Harrison's dingy garage had become a makeshift workshop. One year prior, he bought a neglected 1950 Harley Davidson as a side project. He would work on it during weekends, usually having to redo whatever he had already done at least two more times. Pieces of the old panhead motor were strewn over a sheet he laid out on the filthy concrete floor. Harrison was realistic in believing that it would be something of a small miracle if the thing ever ran again.

He threw on a pair of jeans and boots. He brushed his teeth and wetted down the chunks of hair that were most egregiously sticking up. He looked at himself in the mirror, turning from side to side. Not his whole self, just the squishy middle part. The mid-thirties belly that was slightly protruding over his large American flag belt buckle. His ego started to make a resolution that he would start working out again, shed the extra thirty pounds he had acquired, but he stopped it before it could lie to him. He threw on a long-sleeve shirt and his favorite, worn-out Stetson. An iconic picture of a Midwestern rancher with a discernible New England accent.

First things first: A visit to Edward's General Store to grab a coffee and an egg sandwich, and to pick up a pack of rubber gloves. He would probably banter around with some of the early morning regulars for a few minutes, but he'd be back in time to get a few hours in on the bike before the call into work. He grabbed the keys to his pickup and pulled his phone off the charger next to his bed. It immediately started buzzing in his hand.

"Harrison," he answered. "Yes, I'm at home. No, I'm not sitting. What is it?"

Harrison listened. His knees buckled. He removed his hat and sat on the edge of the bed. Tears welled up in his eyes. When Wells finished speaking, Harrison said the only words he could muster:

"I'm on my way."

20

S canning the pages of local and national media outlets for any mention of Anja's murder, Blake shifted his eyes between the screen of his smartphone and the empty expanse of the lot behind the abandoned foundry. He was uneasy about the openness of the location.

The asphalt surrounding the mammoth facility had long since heaved and cracked. A thin layer of sand and dirt obscured the pavement, giving way to a web of tall weeds and dead grass. The frame of a truck and several pieces of rusted industrial equipment sat in shallow depressions of their own making. The gleaming clear coat of the Dodge did not exactly blend in with the environment. He focused his attention on the driveway at the other end of the four-acre lot. He would see them coming.

Blake was not sure how the CEA even knew he existed. In fact, he had been certain they did not. After all, the only two members he encountered did not live long enough to talk about it. But there was always the possibility. A third man waiting outside? Watching as Blake left, covered in blood? Or had they been watching him and Anja for several days before mounting the attack? He had to assume the threat existed and take the appropriate precautions. But if he weren't on their radar, he would have a tremendous tactical advantage.

Blake reclined the seat back farther behind the concealment of the tinted windows. Even in the low late-afternoon sun, the jet-black film applied to the side windows made it impossible to tell if the vehicle was occupied.

Blake glanced at the time displayed on the dash.

Fifteen minutes. Bring me good news, boys.

He navigated to the Alexandria Times website and scanned the posts. Six posts down, past the recap of the high school junior varsity basketball game and a piece about the preservation of a local historic landmark, he found what he was looking for. A farce of an article. A compulsory report, touting vague information about "heavy police activity in the area."

Blake was not surprised that the whole incident would be kept quiet. In his experience, the Federal Government was not fond of publicity, unless it made them look good. Never mind the public safety concern. The general population was happy to be in the dark. The IPFG massacre had faded from the headlines in less than two days, and that tiny part of the world slipped back into normalcy. But not for him. Not for Anja.

He heard the whine of the motor before he saw the nineties Ford Ranger around the corner toward the back of the building. It stopped abruptly, halfway into the lot. Blake watched intently, holding out for the possibility that Fezz and Khat had taken the extra precaution of switching vehicles. The Agency always had a rotating stockpile of auction vehicles, turned over on an almost weekly basis.

Blake watched as the passenger door of the light pickup swung open and a gaunt young woman spilled out onto the ground. She was wearing a tight purple dress, which barely reached her thighs, and a pair of stiletto high heels that must have been five inches tall. She leapt up and scooped her gold clutch off the ground. Through the window of the open passenger side door, Blake could see the woman shaking her head. Her thick black hair swung across her face. She slammed the door and looked directly at the gleaming Dodge Challenger as if she had spotted a long-lost friend. She started running toward him.

What the hell is this now?

The woman slipped and stumbled on the pointy heels of her shoes, careening toward him with a pathetic prance. Blake held still behind the black tints.

The pickup truck squealed as it looped around the lot, lining up with the woman. The driver gunned the engine and accelerated toward her. At the last second, the pickup swerved and skidded to a stop, missing her by a foot.

A stocky man in his late twenties or early thirties staggered out of the truck. He wore a grease-covered work shirt, sported a wide pornstache, and had a blue bandanna tied around his forehead. He grabbed the woman by the hair and pushed her head toward the hood of the truck.

That's enough.

Blake forced open the door and stepped out onto the pavement. He leaned back against the door, crossed his arms, and called out, "Let her go!"

Startled by Blake's presence, the man released the woman and spun around toward Blake.

"Who are you?" the man said.

Just by the sight of him, Blake could almost smell the bottle of cheap whiskey the guy must have polished off.

"That's not important. And honestly, I don't particularly care who you are or what your problem is. Just let the lady be, get in your little truck there, and go about doing whatever it is you do."

The man's face turned a deeper shade of red. Without saying another word, he reached into the bed of the truck, pulled out a four-foot piece of steel and started walking toward Blake. The woman retreated to the far side of the pickup and peered over the hood.

"You wanna say somethin' smart-assy now, smartass?" the man slurred.

Blake took a few steps toward the man. If the guy was going to start swinging that hunk of metal, Blake did not want it to be anywhere near his car.

"I'll give you a little advice if you want," Blake said.

The man veered to Blake's left side. Blake casually bladed his body toward him.

"Lose the club, it's too heavy."

An angry, perplexed scowl twisted the man's face.

"I mean, it's unwieldy. Seems like you're a little off balance as it is. Trust me, it's the wrong tool for the job," Blake said with a smile and a patronizing shrug.

"You're the one's gonna need." The man cocked back the metal club and lunged at Blake. With a smooth, snapping motion Blake drove his palm up into the center of the man's face and adeptly stepped out of the way.

The hunk of metal crashed down to the pavement, almost pulling the drunk man down with it.

"See what I mean?" Blake said.

The man bellowed, lifted the weapon, and lunged again.

Blake again drove his palm up into the drunk's nose, crushing the remaining cartilage. Blood exploded out across his cheeks. The piece of metal swung out of his grip and landed a couple of feet away. Blake snapped a third palm strike, landing on the same target.

The man's newly flattened face and the black circles under his eyes conspired with the mustache and bandanna to make him look even more foolish than he did initially. He swayed but managed to ball his fists and raise them in a fighting stance. Blake was impressed at his tenacity.

Blake rubbed his hands together and fixed his eyes on the man's chin, as if picking just the right spot. He moved in step with the man, getting a feel for the timing of his swaying and bobbing movements. Suddenly and decisively, Blake struck. He drove his fist up under the left side of the man's chin, driving the bottom jaw and teeth against the top. He crumpled to the ground, unconscious.

Blake picked up the man's limp arms and dragged him across the pebbles and weeds. He propped him up against the back wheel of the pickup. He was snoring loudly. A rhythmic, flappy snore that Blake had become well accustomed to.

Blake squatted down, pulled the man's arm over his shoulder, and hoisted him into the bed of the pickup. Blake walked over to pick up the piece of scrap metal.

"Thank you, mister," the woman said, across the hood of the truck.

"No problem," Blake replied as he laid the steel against the driver's seat and let it rest on the accelerator. The idling motor sang out a half-step higher.

"Step back," Blake said.

The woman took several steps away from the truck.

Blake reached in and shifted the pickup into drive. It started rolling, picking up speed as it veered across the lot at about ten miles an hour toward a chain-link fence at the deepest part of the lot. Just missing a rusted dumpster, the truck crashed through the fence and dipped into the gully separating the industrial property from the surrounding woods. The woman cautiously approached Blake.

"That guy was a jerk. He was trying to take his money back. It's not my fault he was too drunk to get it up." The woman came close and put her hand on Blake's chest. "If you want, I can thank you properly. My treat," she said as she ran her hand downward.

Blake forcefully snatched her wrist and held it tight.

"Listen to me closely. Take those ridiculous shoes off your feet and start walking," Blake said, releasing her wrist. "You're not going to want to be here when your friend wakes up."

Dejected, the woman slipped off her shoes and started walking toward the driveway, stopping only for a moment to shoot Blake an unappreciative sneer. Blake returned to his car and sat down, watching as the woman eventually rounded the corner.

Moments later, a Ford sedan rolled into the lot. As the car approached, Blake could make out the faces of his comrades.

It's about time.

Blake started the car and rolled down the window. As the sedan pulled alongside, Blake noticed a third man, one he did not recognize, sitting in the back seat behind Khat. Khat spoke with excitement from the driver's seat.

"It's on, Mick. It's *on!* Wait till you get a load of this," he said.

Blake ripped a piece of paper from a small notepad and scribbled down an address.

"Gotta move. Meet me here in twenty. Long story," Blake said, handing off the note. He threw the car in gear and stomped the gas, leaving behind a cloud of sand and dust.

As Blake passed the dilapidated guard booth and started making a right onto the roadway, he saw a green four-by-four with monster-sized tires pulled over to the side of the road, a block in the other direction. The waif of a woman, shoes still in hand, was pulling herself up into the passenger seat.

Blake flicked on the radio and cranked up the volume. With a Stone Temple Pilots song blaring, he sped off toward the freeway.

21

Blake drove through the development. Houses in various stages of construction lined the streets. Some already sided, some merely framed, they tapered off to only foundations and empty lots. Blake turned down a dead-end street toward a freshly paved cul-de-sac. The lots that surrounded the circle had not yet been cleared, giving the spot an eerie road-to-nowhere feel.

Blake parked and stepped out of the car. The sun was no longer visible behind the tall trees, and the temperature had dropped a noticeable fifteen degrees. Reaching into the passenger seat to grab his leather jacket, he put it on, feeling the weight of the pistol tugging on the left side. Then he waited.

Khat, Fezz, and their plus-one pulled in a few minutes behind him. The three men exited the car and joined Blake, standing in a loose circle. The stranger carried a manila folder.

"Mick, this is Griff," Fezz said. "Former hot-shot Navy pilot. He's been with us for about eight months. Good people. Griff, the legendary Mick."

Blake extended his hand and Griff shook it with vigor. The swarthy man was obviously younger than Blake and his two close friends. He had a broad chest and buoyant air that made him instantly likable.

"Griff is sort of our new you," Khat said.

"Hey now, let's not get carried away," Griff said. "I've heard the war stories."

Yep. I like this guy.

"Griff does all the heavy lifting when it comes to the cyber stuff, we brought him in to help us help you to work *Logos*. Damn good thing we did. Fezz and I could never have gotten what Griff got in ten hours," Khat said.

"If you're wondering if you can trust him, believe me, after what went down in Lebanon, I can guarantee it," Fezz added, wrapping his hand around the back of Griff's neck and shaking, affectionately.

"Did these *jamokes* give you the name Griff?" Blake pried.

"Um. No. It's my name. Griffin," he replied matter-of-factly.

"Well that's boring. Never met a fighter pilot without a call sign," Blake said.

"Helicopters," Griff corrected, "and my call sign is Apollo."

"Yeah, we're definitely not calling him that," Khat protested.

"Not a chance." Fezz added.

"Why ya gotta break his balls?" Blake asked. He knew why. It was a sign that they liked him. That they meant it when they said they trusted him. It was all the endorsement Blake needed. "Griff, did the boys ever tell you how they got their names?"

A smile appeared on Fezz's face. Khat had the opposite reaction.

"Fezz told me it was something to do with Andre the Giant. About some movie," Griff recalled.

"The Princess Bride," Blake said, emphatically. " We used to recite the whole thing word for word. Watch it and tell me this big oaf is not a spitting image of Fezzik." Blake laughed.

Khat cracked a smile. They all knew Fezz was nowhere near the size of Andre the Giant. But there was still a resemblance.

"But more importantly, what about Khat?" Blake asked.

"No, he never said." Griff's demeanor showed a mild apprehension, worried he was being unwittingly roped into something.

"Oh, this is good, " Blake started. "We were in Somalia, right? In this safe house. We were setting up to interrogate these three guys we captured, and we were standing by, waiting for the interpreter. When we picked them up, we took this big bundle of khat off one of them."

"You know what that is, right?" Fezz interrupted.

Griff nodded.

Blake continued. "So, we're screwing around and Fezz starts busting Khat's balls that he won't try the stuff. So Khat takes this huge wad of leaves and stuffs it in his mouth. Within a minute he started turning green, but he was committed at that point so he wouldn't just spit it out. Then he just pukes. I mean projectile vomits directly in the face of one of the prisoners."

Blake and Fezz roared with laughter. Griff joined in, laughing mostly at the contagious uproar of the others. Even Khat gave a reluctant chuckle.

"Ha, ha. It never gets old with you two," Khat said.

Blake spoke through his laughter. "The guy was tied to a chair so he couldn't wipe off his face, he just looked confused, like he wanted to say, '*why*?'"

Fezz and Blake broke out in raucous laughter once more.

"We were laughing like buffoons. Even the other two prisoners started laughing. None of them spoke a lick of English so they all must have thought we were either complete imbeciles or absolutely crazy."

The laughter continued, eventually dying down to a few sporadic chuckles, sighs, and groans.

"Whatever they thought, it probably helped. They broke easily," Fezz recalled.

"Yep. We got the info we needed. And Khat's been Khat ever since," Blake said.

"Alright, alright," Khat forced his way back into the conversation.

"Griff's fully up to speed now. Can we talk about what we came up with?"

Blake was acutely aware that the men had information. Information that his one-track mind desperately wanted. But he had consciously forced himself to let it go, briefly. To allow himself a moment of levity. It was what they had always done. To counteract the horrors with stupid, often twisted, humor. A universal coping mechanism that all men in their position shared.

"Give it to me," Blake said.

"Griff," Khat deferred.

Griff opened the folder. "I ran the criteria through the database and narrowed it down to about two dozen possible locations. All churches or religious sites that are no longer in operation, all within a two-hundred-fifty-mile radius of D.C., and all sitting on at least an acre of land. I figured I'd go back and expand the radius if none of the spots panned out but, as it turned out, there was no need. I pulled access to *Logos* and ran the algorithms against the possibilities. I had it go back four months, analyzing movement, traffic, heat signatures, the works. I came up with a couple of standouts. Peculiar activity where there shouldn't have been much at all. One of the places turned out to be under renovation. That checked out. But this other one?"

Griff passed Blake a map and a photograph of a stone structure with a huge wooden door that came to a point at the top. Although the paint had almost completely chipped away, Blake could tell that it had once been a bright red color.

Griff continued. "An old stone Evangelical church that was part of a swath of land taken over by the state to build a highway that never came to fruition. There was periodic vehicular traffic in and out of the area, including a delivery truck that arrived every Saturday morning like clockwork. Two men would wheel handcarts, stacked with boxes, back and forth. And, get this, fast forward to last Monday. Two vehicles pulled up at around six o'clock in the morning. The driver of one vehicle got into the other and drove off. Four people, wearing hoods, came out of the building and got into the car that was left there. If you give me another day of processing, I could probably get you pretty good pictures of their faces."

"This is your church, Mick. It's gotta be," Fezz said.

"There's one other thing. A big thing," Khat said, as if intentionally building the suspense.

"I'm listening," Blake said.

"The property was sold off by the state a few years back. The church and several surrounding acres were bought by a company named Halidom. Records show the original owner of the company was Ray Cosh," Khat explained. "It turns out, Ray Cosh was former Chief Technology Officer of, you guessed it, IPFG."

"You're kidding me," Blake said.

"Not kidding. Cosh reportedly died in a car crash five years ago while traveling on IPFG business. Milburn himself spoke about the incident in a press conference. The company's official release says that Cosh was attending a meeting in northern California. Supposedly, the rented Porsche he was driving left the Pacific Coast Highway and tumbled eighty feet down a cliff onto the rocky shore. The car caught fire and burned down to the frame, but Cosh's body was not recovered. The article assumed Cosh was ejected and lost to the Pacific currents," Khat said.

"Lines up perfectly with what your source told you," Fezz added. "The burns, the bank, all of it."

"If Ray Cosh is our *Metus*, Milburn knows more than he's telling the FBI," Blake said.

"It's possible, but there's still a lot of ifs," said Khat.

"All right then. I'm paying our friends a visit tomorrow morning, before dawn. You guys still in?" Blake asked.

"I'm good," Fezz said, without hesitation.

"Me too," Khat followed.

"Griff," Blake said, "you think you can get up on the satellites in real time tonight? Give us a bit of intel while we're out there?"

"Sure," Griff said.

Blake could tell that Griff was at least a little disappointed that he was not invited to join the assault team. But Blake was sure that he would appreciate the lack of exposure if things went sideways.

"You guys go get geared up." Blake pointed to the map. "Echo is right here, only about two miles from the target. We'll meet there at twenty-three hundred hours. That'll give us time to get set up on the place. Everyone set your phone to share your location with the group. Griff will be able to track us and give us a heads-up in case we're missing something."

The men thumbed through their devices and set up the group sharing. Blake loved leveraging consumer technology in this way. It nearly replaced the bulky, expensive equipment they used to have to beg, borrow, or steal. Griff's access and skill with *Logos*, however, could not be replaced.

The men headed to their cars.

"We're gonna get an hour or two of shut-eye before all hell breaks loose," Fezz said. "You should do the same. You look like crap."

"Thanks," Blake said, "but there's someone I have to see."

22

"**D**id she call you back?" Wells asked.

Harrison finished chewing the bite of the cheeseburger while closing the lid of the Styrofoam takeout container.

"She did. The lab pretty much confirmed what we already knew," Harrison finally said. "Nuria was able to put together a rough timeline based on the blood spatter. They also looked at the ballistics and she said there's no doubt a fourth person killed the two bastards. There was no stippling and the angles were inconsistent with self-inflicted wounds. She said there wouldn't be an official report for another week or so."

"How about DNA, fingerprints?" Wells asked.

"Apparently, she's got no pull with the Bio department. But I did get in touch with Hayes myself. He said they're trying to fast-track the swabs and the latents. Even still, there's eighty-three items to process. It's going to be a while. Other than that, we just have the two witnesses left. Meg's interviewing them now."

"What about the church thing? Have we gotten anywhere with that?" Wells asked.

"Maybe. Yes. You remember the abandoned one I was showing you? Spence went out there and spoke to the neighbor just east. He's got about 30 acres out there. The guy said there's not supposed to be anyone on the property of the old church, but he's seen cars coming and going late at night. Spence and Taylor checked it out and said that there's a gate on the driveway and it was wide open. The latch was broken off, with the lock still attached. He took pictures. There were tons of *No Trespassing* signs posted. He said he and Taylor walked down to the building to look around. They even knocked. No answer, of course. But he swears he heard movement inside."

"Do you think that's the place? Couldn't it just be homeless squatters?" Wells asked.

"Possibly. But if it were squatters, there probably wouldn't be regular vehicular traffic. Plus, it lines up too nicely. The remote location, the inexplicable activity. It would have helped immensely if we knew who Anja's informant was. We're trying to get in touch with the owner of the property but having trouble following the paper trail. It's still apparently owned by some company, but we can't find a contact or even a physical address for them. Hudson's working on that now. I have a meeting with the AUSA to see if he thinks we have enough for a search. We might have to stretch it a bit, but it might fly."

"It might. We could get a little latitude on this one, especially with an imminent threat of another attack. It would look extremely bad on the Bureau and U.S. Attorney's Office if we don't get to them in time," Wells speculated. "Just make sure the local PD stays clear of the place. The last thing we want to do is spook them into fleeing before we can crash the place. Assuming Spence and Taylor haven't done that already."

"Sorry to interrupt," Special Agent Armon Grasso said, seemingly coming out of nowhere. "This just came over the fax for you. From the ME's office." He handed the documents to Harrison.

Harrison flipped through the four pages and returned to the coversheet; a handwritten message scrawled across the *Office of the Chief Medical Examiner* letterhead.

"It says they performed a sexual assault kit on Anja and found evidence that Anja recently had sexual intercourse." Harrison struggled to speak over the lump that was forming in his throat.

He read verbatim: "While we found no internal or external injury further indicating forcible rape, we cannot rule out the possibility. Viable male DNA samples have been recovered and are being forwarded to the Department of Forensic Science. Kits conducted on the two male subjects showed no signs of sexual activity. Blood samples are being sent for use in DNA comparison."

"Lord Jesus, she was raped? Animals." Wells grumbled.

"It makes no sense. Three bad guys come in, one rapes Anja, then shoots his two accomplices, and then shoots Anja through a wall and covers her body in a towel? What are we missing here?"

"Maybe it was consensual," Wells said. "Maybe she hooked up with someone. We don't know what she did on her own time."

"You seriously think she had a one-night stand with an Evangelist, who invited along two of his buddies?" The frustration was evident in Harrison's voice.

"Come on Harrison, don't be an ass. I'm just saying maybe our third party was someone unrelated to this case, who happened to be in the wrong place at the wrong time. Someone with some training or military experience. I mean, that could describe half the men in this town. Maybe the guy had to fight his way out and took off because he was afraid he'd be in trouble." Wells stopped himself from spiraling off on a tangent. "I'm just trying to keep an open mind. You should too. We both cared about her, I just want to get this right."

Harrison furtively grappled with his emotions. They all cared about Anja, just as they cared about one another. But, for him, it was different. Wells couldn't have known about the feelings he had developed for Anja. No one could have. Especially not Anja. He had put great effort into masking it, only admiring her from a distance.

He always seized the time he was able to spend with her, even if it were only in a professional capacity. There were times when he considered ignoring his better judgment and telling her how he felt, but he lost the nerve before he could get the words out.

He told himself that he did not want to ruin a good working relationship, but it was fear of rejection that paralyzed him. Anja was out of his league, he knew that. She would have laughed in his face; he was sure of it. But he wished, with the deep ache of regret, that she was there to shoot him down.

Special Agent Meg Huovinen, a five-foot-two powerhouse of a personality, emerged from one of five small interview rooms, situated directly behind Harrison's chair. Huovinen shook her head.

"Nothing good?" Wells asked.

"Nothing great. This one says she looked out her window around the time the 911 came into the PD. She says she saw a guy with a beard walking away from Anja's. At first, she said she thought he was a dark-skinned Hispanic male, then she changed it to white guy with red hair who looked like a zombie. Then she said it was dark and she wasn't really sure. She couldn't remember anything else about him. The other witness, did you see him, the elderly guy with the lazy eye? That guy said that he brought his dog out and saw the *blonde woman* fighting with *one of them* in the street. I thought maybe he was talking about the Evangelists. Nope. Turns out he was referring to the visitors. From outer space!"

"Alright, thanks Meg." Harrison stood up and grabbed his blazer. "I'm heading out to this meeting. I'll keep you updated."

"Bring me good news," Wells said, as Harrison disappeared into the hallway.

23

"**M**r. Milburn's office," Sheryl Pannikin answered.

Blake knew that Milburn's assistant was not in the office. On a Saturday night at a quarter after seven, the last thing Pannikin probably wanted to do was field work calls. But she dutifully answered her company cell phone anyway.

"Hi, Sheryl. I'm sorry, I'm just calling to clarify Mr. Milburn's reservation for this evening," Blake said. He spoke in a high, rhythmic tone.

"Mr. Milburn will be there at eight o'clock. Is there a problem?" she asked.

"Oh no. No problem at all. It's just that I'm looking at the reservation and, well this is embarrassing, we seem to have neglected to note which location."

"What do you mean?" Sheryl said. Blake could hear the distraction in her voice and the murmur of voices in the background.

"Since we opened the new place last weekend, it's been an absolute frenzy. I just want to make sure we're prepared for Mr. Milburn's party, you know. I didn't want to assume."

"Honestly, I didn't even know there was a new one." Sheryl said.

"Oh. It's fabulous darling. It's called *Petit*. Chef Laurent is an artiste. Believe me, the Oeuf Cocotte d'Escargot is to die for."

"Sounds great, I'm sure. But Mr. Milburn specifically said La Tavola," she interrupted. "Party of three. Please tell me we're all set with this, I booked it over a week ago."

"It's all set darling, La Tavola it is. Ciao."

Blake hung up the phone, opened his mapping app, and tapped in *La Tavola*.

He snaked his way through city traffic, circled the block and, after three passes, found parking on G Street.

A quick Google image search returned several recent pictures of Milburn. He selected one and studied it, making sure he could easily identify him in a crowd.

Blake got out of the car, walked back toward Fifteenth and paced around, keeping an eye out for Milburn to arrive.

At ten minutes before eight, a taxi pulled up and stopped in front of La Tavola. A man stepped out. Blake immediately recognized him from the images. Milburn buttoned his jacket and headed toward the restaurant. The doorman greeted him and swung open the gilded entryway. Milburn disappeared inside.

By the way Milburn carried himself, the way he walked, the way he ignored the doorman, Blake could sense his arrogance.

The driver pulled away, but Blake hung back for a minute to allow time for Milburn to be seated. Blake could only hope that Milburn arrived before his guests and not the other way around. He only needed a few minutes.

Blake moved to the entrance. The doorman swung open the heavy door. Blake thanked him and slid inside, bypassing the coat check and moving directly toward the dining room. The maître d' called after him:

"Sir, can I help you?" he said.

Blake stopped in the entrance to the dining room, scanning the dimly lit tables for his target. Without looking back, he replied, "I'm supposed to be meeting someone. Oh, I see them. Thanks." He walked into the room with purpose.

Blake was halfway across the restaurant when he spotted Milburn sitting at a table with four chairs and two empty place settings, situated in the far corner of the room.

The restaurant was busy, nearly full. But the patrons, including Milburn himself, were so consumed with their menus, their appetizers, their witty conversations, they had not given Blake a second glance.

He moved through the crowd, squeezing between the small spaces separating the backs of unrelated diners. As soon as he reached Milburn's table, he sat. Directly across from him.

"Mr. Milburn, what a surprise," Blake said.

"Ah... yes, indeed." Milburn's face was tattooed with surprise. But deeper than that, it projected a precarious confusion.

Blake could tell the wheels were turning in his head. Grinding out an inner monologue consisting of a hundred overlapping questions. *Do I know this person? Am I supposed to know this person? Why don't I remember? Where did I meet him? Was it a friendly encounter? Is he important? Did I promise him something?*

When it came to his personal life, Blake himself had been in the same predicament more times than he could count. But the stakes were different for a man like Milburn. For Blake, it was an awkward moment that he would laugh off and jokingly attribute to his ADD. For Milburn, it could mean multimillion-dollar deals going south. Powerful feathers being ruffled.

"I'll save you the drama. You don't know me. I don't know you. We've never met," Blake said.

Milburn's spine straightened. The bravado rushed back into his flaccid shell, puffing him up like a balloon.

"In that case, please remove yourself from my table. Immediately. Before I have you removed."

"Sorry, but that's not going to happen," Blake said. "Not until we have a little chat about the robbery on L Street."

"Enough of this," Milburn spat. "Waiter." Milburn caught the attention of a waiter who was taking the order of an older couple three tables away.

The waiter motioned to Milburn, indicating that he would tend to him in a moment.

"Ray Cosh," Blake said.

He delivered the words deliberately and then carefully studied Milburn's face for micro-expressions. Blake often used his training in reading the small, involuntary flashes of facial movement to detect deception or suppressed emotional response. Milburn's outward appearance remained stoic. Completely unfazed. But Blake could see the underlying nervous energy churning inside of him.

The waiter hurried over.

"Yes, sir. Your martini will be right out. I apologize for the wait. Is there anything else I can get for you, sir?"

Blake gambled that he had hit a nerve by mentioning the name of Milburn's old colleague. People always wonder why criminal suspects will sit and answer questions for hours, instead of simply walking away. It is because they want to know what the interrogator knows. Their chaotic mind needs to know. Milburn was no different.

Blake pointed to the waiter with only a flick of his head and looked Milburn in the eye. "Go on then," he goaded.

"Bring my friend one as well, would you?" Milburn said. He picked up his phone, held it in front of his face, and swiped at the screen. "It looks like my other associates are running a bit behind, I'll wait to order until they arrive," Milburn said, without taking his eyes off the screen. He continued manipulating the device, rudely signaling the waiter that he was done with him.

"Right away sir," he said, scurrying off toward the bar area.

Milburn took a long expansive breath and exhaled loudly. He put his phone on the table and leaned in. "Ray Cosh is dead."

"I think you know that's not true. I think you know Cosh was responsible for the attack on your bank," Blake said. "What is it that you're not telling the FBI? What does he have against you? Innocent people are dead. Someone extremely close to me is dead. For what? For what!?" Blake slammed his fist down on the table. He caught himself and looked around, hoping he had not been as disruptive as he felt.

"Look, I don't know who you are or what you have to do with any of this. But Ray Cosh died in a traffic accident. I don't know what else to tell you. Now, I'm going to have to insist that you take your conspiracy theories and leave. Do not bother me again with this garbage."

Blake leaned in. He spoke faintly, the low register lending a gravelly quality to his voice. "Listen to me closely. If I find out that there is something you're not telling me, believe me, you will wish you had."

"I'll be sure to keep that in mind. Now, if you don't mind." Milburn paused. "Or I can simply call the police and have you removed."

Blake stood up and placed his hands on the table. "Thank you. You've been most helpful," he said, facetiously. "You enjoy the rest of your evening." *Prick.*

Blake left quickly, passing the waiter balancing two martini glasses on a silver tray.

Milburn picked up his phone and scrolled through the contacts. He pressed the screen to dial and raised the phone to his ear.

The waiter arrived to deliver the cocktails. Milburn motioned for him to leave the drinks as the call connected.

"Robert, it's me," Milburn said. "We've got a whole new issue. I'm sending you a picture of a man. Find out who he is. I'm not sure how much he knows, but he most definitely knows about Cosh."

He listened to the response.

"Okay. Sending it now."

Milburn texted the image he had managed to take of Blake and put the phone back on the table. He picked up a martini in each hand. One after the other, he sucked them down in two desperate gulps.

147

24

Blake checked his watch. Twenty-two hundred hours. He removed it from his wrist and placed it on the dresser next to Anja's business card. He picked up the card, turned it over, and gazed at the handwritten number on the back.

He realized that the number, written in her own hand, was the only thing in his possession that had any connection to her. After all, he abandoned any shared belongings that remained when he moved out of their town house, nine years prior. At the time, Blake wanted a fresh start with nothing to remind him of her. Now, he would give anything to be reminded.

He held the card up to his nose and inhaled, hoping to smell her. To sense her. But he found nothing except the uninspiring smell of ink. He put the card in the pocket of his jeans.

You're coming along for this one, Jo.

Blake rifled through the black duffel bag, double-checking that all his desired equipment was there. Satisfied with the items he originally included in the go-bag, he zipped it up and slung it over his shoulder. He grabbed his jacket and shut off the bedroom light.

Before opening the front door, he set the alarm system to "Armed

Away." A rhythmic beeping signaled that the thirty-second arming countdown had begun. He stepped out onto the stoop, locked the door, and headed to the car parked on the street two car lengths from the front stairs.

Blake moved to the car, running through his mental checklist. Replaying the plan, over and over. Trying to consider every possible scenario.

The truth was that there was no solid plan. He had rushed to action. He had thrown away all the experience he gained in his career. All the hard-earned lessons of defeat later attributed to an unseen flaw that was missed in the planning stages. Blake knew that what he was about to attempt was stupid, at best. More likely suicidal. And he was tired. So freakin' tired.

He opened the trunk and tossed in the nylon bag. If war was coming, at least he'd be prepared for it.

Although it was after ten o'clock at night, his block was still active. Several people strolled by on the sidewalk. A couple, arm in arm. A group of two men and a woman, dressed for a night on the town, if not underdressed for the weather. They smiled and gave Blake a friendly nod. He wondered what they would think if they knew what was in the bag. Worse, what was in his heart. More dangerous than any stockpile of munitions.

He walked around to the passenger side, opened the door, and placed his jacket on the seat. Despite the chill, he preferred more freedom of movement while he was driving, one of his idiosyncrasies perhaps, but he had long since stopped cataloging them.

He touched his pockets, front and back, and gave his mind one last attempt to recall what he could be forgetting. His phone and some cash were in his pants pockets. His pistol was in his jacket. Night vision, ammunition, in the bag.

Flash bangs. Of course.

In one of Blake's imaginary run-throughs, he considered making a loud entry. If that scenario became necessary, he would need the concussion grenades. He decided it would be worth the delay as he would have to run back inside.

He swung the car door closed with a familiar thud. His subconscious registered another sound, layered over the metallic creak and dampened suction sound of the weather stripping, but his conscious mind did not have time to catch up. The sound of boots shuffling across concrete.

The world turned black in an instant.

He felt the tugging at his neck as he heard the distinct ratcheting sound of the zip tie. He clawed at his face, trying to find a weakness in the heavy fabric bag that enveloped his head.

In the half second it took Blake to get his bearings, his mind generated a hundred thoughts. How could he have been so foolish and let his guard down? He was fully aware of the possibility they were watching him. Waiting for him to present an opportunity. And he had given it to them. He was supposed to bring the reckoning, not the other way around. But he could still breathe.

The zip tie was fastened tight enough to make it impossible to slip the bag off his head but not so tight that it cut off his air or the blood flow to his brain. That was something. And if they really wanted to kill him, why not just shoot him from behind. No, they wanted to take him. He could work with that. Even blind, he could fight them off. At least long enough for some bystander to happen by.

Just hold them off.

Blake swung his elbow, connecting with soft, meaty tissue. He felt a jerk and, disoriented by the inability to see his surroundings, lost his balance and tumbled toward the ground.

He felt the sudden shift in momentum in his inner ear before the pain. A burning ache that radiated out from the back of his head. He had no idea what he had hit, but it was decidedly hard. Sprawled out on the ground, he successfully fought to remain alert.

"Grab his arms," one of the men said.

"I'm trying," said another. "You get his legs."

As soon as he felt the hands wrap around his ankles, Blake snapped back his feet and kicked upwards.

"O of." The groan let Blake know he had caused at least some damage. Probably not enough.

Blake listened hard, trying to translate the noises into a mental picture of his attackers' positions.

He listened but heard nothing more until the unforgiving steel slide of a pistol slammed into the side of his head and set off the screeching ring in his ears. He tried to push himself off the ground, but his body refused to obey. He struggled to make sense of the situation. How long had he been down? Was he dreaming? One by one, his senses went quiet as he drifted in and out of consciousness.

He felt the weightlessness of being lifted, he thought. He heard the slamming of the trunk above him, didn't he? It would not matter. The intensity of the urge to sleep entangled him and finally dragged him to its depths.

25

"Don't touch that." Fezz batted Khat's hand away from the tuning knob on the Ford's car stereo.

"Sinead O'Connor, seriously?" Khat said. "I'm embarrassed to know you right now."

"What's wrong with Sinead?" Fezz turned up the volume. "I haven't heard this song in forever. Reminds me of a bus trip to D.C. that I went on in the eighth grade. For two days, they drove us around to see crap we didn't care about. National Archives. Smithsonian. The Capitol. Every time we would get back on that coach bus, this song was playing. Whatever station that driver listened to was playing this thing on a loop. Every time I hear it, it brings back memories. Mostly of making out with Becky Urnst in the back of the bus."

"The song still sucks." Khat spun the dial in search of something worth listening to. After auditioning a few stations, he found nothing. "Where the hell is Mick?"

"He'll be here."

"He's five minutes late. When is Mick ever late?"

There was no need for a response. They both knew the answer was *never*.

A silence fell over the passenger compartment. Both men stared out the windshield at the lake. The trees swayed. Ripples moved across the reflection of the moonlight, which streaked through the black water as if it were trying to touch them.

Tragedy, loss, sacrifice. Those things came with the mission. With the calling. But the festering doubt they promoted did not live in the moments of terror. Not in the gunfight or narrow escape. Not in the rushing air of a high altitude jump or the discomfort of a foxhole. No. It lived in the quiet, serene moments. The moments when the mind had the time and space to finally make the connections. To consider the gravity.

"He's not taking it well," Khat finally said.

"No. He's not. But he'll be all right. He's just gonna need time. You know how he felt about her."

Khat nodded.

"We've all gotta work this kinda stuff out in our own way. Remember when Bonzo died. After we got home, you, me, and Mick went to that place with the street signs hanging all over the walls. I forget the name of that place. Anyway, you got all cocked up and slugged that random dude who was just sitting there minding his own business. Then you said, 'That was for Bonzo.' The guy was like 'Who the hell is Bonzo?' Grief does weird stuff, man."

"It did make me feel better."

"Didn't make me feel better. It started a wild brawl. Blake and I had to fend off twenty dudes to get you out of there."

"It wasn't twenty dudes. It was like four," Khat protested.

"Okay. Maybe twelve," Fezz compromised.

"Every time you tell that story the number gets bigger." Khat twisted to look out of the rear window. "Seriously Fezz, I don't like that he's not here yet."

"Give him a call," Fezz suggested.

Khat did. He gave it three attempts but was greeted by Blake's voicemail recording each time.

"Nothing?" Fezz asked. He unlocked his own phone. "Here, we should be able to pull up his location."

The app displayed a mile radius around them. Fezz could see the two dots, placing him and Khat precisely at their location. No Blake. He zoomed out to a twenty-mile radius and swiped his thumb over and over, moving the view closer and closer to Blake's house.

"I don't see him at all," Fezz said. "Not even at his place. Maybe his phone's dead and he lost track of time."

"He texted me and said he was running home quickly and then heading out," Khat explained.

"Text him again. Tell him we're on our way to him. Unless he says otherwise."

"Okay. Just start driving," Khat said. "I'll text him."

Fezz flicked on the headlights and pulled onto the road. He headed back toward Alexandria, expertly handling the car at speeds far too fast for the narrow, windy road. They made the entire thirty-minute trip without receiving a response from Blake.

"His car's here," Khat announced.

"I see that," Fezz drawled. "He must have fallen asleep. I'll stay with the car, you run up to the door."

Khat hopped out, ran up the steps, and rang the bell. He smiled and waved at the miniature camera mounted inside the doorbell housing, "Wake up."

There was no response. Khat rang a few more times. He turned back to Fezz and shrugged.

Fezz shut off the car and stepped out. He walked to Blake's car and looked through the driver's side window. Khat came down off the steps and did the same on the passenger side.

"His jacket is in there," Fezz said.

Khat tried the door. "It's open." He picked up the jacket and immediately felt the sagging weight of the pistol and suppressor. "I told you something was wrong."

"Check the pockets for his phone," Fezz instructed.

He did.

"No, nothing," Khat said. "Look him up on the app again."

Fezz walked around to the sidewalk. He and Khat stood side-by-side, hovering over the screen of Fezz's phone.

"Look," Fezz said, as if trying to solicit a second opinion. "No signal in this area." He dragged the screen a few times until the map covered the meeting spot. "Or in this area."

"Zoom out more," Khat said.

Fezz did but only their own two dots were visible.

"More. Zoom out more," Khat urged.

Fezz zoomed out until the map covered a hundred-mile radius. There, forty miles in the opposite direction from the meeting spot, was Blake's dot.

Fezz looked at Khat in a way that made Khat want to check that his nose hadn't fallen off.

"Fezz?"

Fezz ground his teeth, "Get in the car."

26

Blake was floating. Bobbing gently with each passing wave. He could feel the light of the sun warming his face. His cheek pulsing. It was making a soft, rhythmic sound. He tried to ignore the sensation, to consider it a slight inconvenience, as his body pulled at him to return to deep slumber. *Five more minutes, just five —more.* The dull thumping sound morphed like an envelope filter, rising to a high treble. *Whap. Whap. Whap.* The pulsing grew to a jarring pain. The rhythm seemed to double.

His eyes abruptly shot open but reflexively squinted again at the brain-searing light. The world came flooding back to him as he rolled his head away from the incessant slapping.

"There you are," a man's voice said.

Blake forced his eyes open and quickly adjusted to the light. His eyes connected and locked, almost magnetically, with those that hovered over him, peering out through two holes cut into a grotesque mask. A few days ago, he wouldn't have been disgusted by the plastic prop. But that was then. Now, he felt the debilitating hatred climb up from his core. *Don't feel, think.*

Blake felt the cold metal of the table on the bare skin of his back.

He had been stripped of his clothing and was lying on an incline with his head toward the floor. The blood, flowing with gravity toward his aching skull, wasn't helping the splitting headache that he had finally become acutely aware of.

He tried to stretch his arms. Although he could lift them up, they were bound together at the wrists. More problematic, he considered, was that his ankles were each bound to the top of the stainless-steel slab by a thick leather strap, the kind Blake imagined would be used by demented orderlies in some old-timey insane asylum. He didn't particularly like the feeling of the sterile metal beneath him either.

It's like the goddamn morgue.

"We're going to have a little discussion. Hopefully, a very brief discussion. For your sake," the man said.

Focus.

Blake took a deep breath and blinked slowly. Deliberately. He opened his eyes and allowed himself to see. All of it.

There were three men in the room. Two masked men stood silently on either side of a metal door. There were no windows, but the door didn't look to have deadbolts or other reinforcements.

One way out.

The two men by the door were not particularly large, but they were clearly fit. Like their more talkative counterpart, they were dressed in blue jeans and black, hooded sweatshirts. The hoods were pulled up, sealing off any view of their faces from the side. Blake noticed that both stood in almost the same posture: hands behind their backs, legs slightly spread apart. *Parade Rest.* These guys had some military experience. Guys get so used to relaxing into this posture that it becomes second nature.

The man hovering over him was heavier but noticeably softer. The shape of the black hoodie bulged out in nearly the opposite configuration as the more muscular sentries posted by the door. This was no tweaker off the street. He was well-spoken in the little he said, and he gave the impression that he was older, probably a little older than Blake. His voice, muffled through the narrow slit in the painted mouth of the mask, was not high-pitched, but it did lack a booming, authoritative quality.

Tubs and his two sidekicks.

At his angle, Blake could see clearly behind him, but was blind to anything past his feet.

As far as he could tell, the room was empty with the rather notable exception of the five watering cans lined up on the floor, a few feet from his head. The green plastic cans had long spouts and could probably hold two or three gallons of liquid, the kind of thing you take out to your patio to water the flowers.

These guys aren't gardeners.

Blake knew all too well what the sum of the scene meant to him. He had been waterboarded on more than one occasion: first in SERE training and again when he joined the agency. The classified program he endured the second time around made SERE training get re-filed in his brain from the trauma bin to the part where you store the more pleasant stuff. Blake sighed audibly at the prospect of having to endure round three.

All right, Tubs. Let's do this.

"What do you want?" Blake asked pointedly.

"It's simple. I want to know what you know," the fat man replied.

"I know that two-thirds of the world's eggplant is grown in New Jersey. How about that, eh? Did you know that?"

Blake barely saw the fat man's fist raise up before it was crashing into his jaw. The pain peaked and quickly subsided to a throbbing ache. His assailant motioned to the other two, who rushed toward the table.

Blake saw the one on the left stretch a dark-colored cloth between his hands before bringing the cloth down forcefully over the entirety of his face, forcing him back into the surreal darkness. But this time, Blake was not bobbing around in a dream. He was in full control.

Blake writhed and squirmed as the sentry tried to hold the cloth tight to his face. He made unintelligible noises that he knew would be muffled by the wet cloth sealing off his mouth. It would be what they expected.

And then, it came. The cold water rushing into his nostrils. Blake fought the urge to gasp for breath as the water filled his sinuses and pooled at the back of his throat.

You know you're not drowning. You know how this works.

Blake focused on the words and tried to fight off the panic. He was always amazed that no matter how many times he had been through this, no matter how many rounds of desensitization training he had endured, he was always millimeters away from succumbing to the panic. Succumbing to the churning, raging fear.

Blake held his breath. He knew it had only been a half a minute or so, even though it felt like more. He let his body tense and spasm. His captors would believe the technique was effective if they sensed his body naturally railing against its own death.

Then, it stopped.

"How about now?" the fat man said with a newfound air of confidence. "Anything smart to say?"

"Okay. Okay," Blake stammered deliberately. "Just don't do it again."

Blake and his team had used this same technique to varying effect on several occasions. There was a rhythm to it. A cadence.

These guys are doing it wrong.

Relief washed over him.

Tubs is an amateur.

Blake could almost feel his core, his soul, hardening to a dense steel. He no longer had a doubt that he could outlast his abuser, but he knew they would eventually grow tired. They would eventually decide to kill him.

"We know you've been snooping around. What did you find? That's all I need to know. You tell me that and you walk out that door. If not, well, then I hope you don't drown before coming to your senses."

By how the fat man phrased the question "What did you find?",

Blake calculated that the three amateurs didn't know much about his past, if anything at all. To them, he must have been an aging software engineer with too much curiosity. A monkey that mistakenly opened the wrong digital doorway. If that were true, he surmised, they probably have not discovered that their compatriots were not coming back with a pulse.

Blake decided not to answer the fat man's question at all. He laid his head back, closed his eyes, and waited.

Think. How the hell do you get out of here?

Behind his eyelids, he pictured himself lying beneath a piece of rusted industrial equipment that had been discarded on a metal platform outside the second level offices of a shipbuilding facility in Kerch. The imagery, recorded in his memory many years before, was as tangible as the table he was bound to.

He could smell damp air. He could feel pressure on his knees and elbows as he lay prone. The metal floor was nothing more than one-inch wide grates which, when he looked down, made him feel like he was suspended thirty feet in the air.

He, Fezz, Khat, and Bonzo had gotten pinned down while trying to exfiltrate with documents Khat located in one of the dingy offices. The four, each huddled in their own dark blind, could see each other across the platform. They laid still for nine hours, only occasionally communicating with each other using hand signals, while dozens of armed, Russian-speaking guards came and went.

The guards gathered in clusters. Smoking, laughing, patrolling. At one point, Blake counted a dozen men on, under, or in sight of the platform where the team had taken up temporary residence. In the end, it was patience that proved the most useful skill. It was waiting for the perfect moment, and being ready to seize it swiftly, without hesitation.

In one instant, a fleeting moment, when all that stood between them and the notion of quietly slipping off into pre-dawn oblivion was one guard. One unsuspecting and unlucky guard. Fezz silently slipped behind the poor kid and snapped his neck. He let the limp body slide down the steep, grated staircase to the ground. An unfortunate accident, his comrades would later say.

After stepping over the contorted corpse and sprinting into the fog, not one of them looked back as they slipped over a chain-link fence and into the undergrowth of an adjacent vacant lot.

Like in Kerch, Blake knew that what he needed was patience. He needed time to let his options unfold. Most of all, he needed to be ever ready to strike.

The memory faded. Blake settled in for a long and trying night as the cold, wet cloth enveloped his world once more.

27

Fezz watched the GPS on his phone, directing Khat on how to approach.

"Pull over here," Khat said.

"Is that it down there?" Fezz asked, as he slowed to a stop and switched off the headlights.

"Has to be," Khat answered, still examining the screen.

They could see the top of a long brick building from the shoulder of the desolate roadway.

"It's some kind of factory," Fezz guessed.

"Google lists it as Brennan Place Industrial Condos. From what I can tell, companies can rent space to use for manufacturing and that kind of thing. The website says each unit has offices, warehouse space, and a loading dock."

"Great, now we have to find out which one he's in. Are you sure he's inside?" Fezz questioned.

"I think so. It looks like the last known location that was logged before the phone lost contact with the tower was right here."

Khat pointed out a small blue dot that was overlaid on a satellite image of the building. The dot appeared to be well inside the perimeter of the structure.

"Even if this thing is a little off, he's gotta be in either this unit or that one," Khat pointed out.

Khat noticed, from the overhead view, what looked like two or three steps jutting out from the building at regular intervals along one side. He assumed that the steps represented the main entrance to each individual unit.

"Let's go take a look," Fezz suggested.

Khat agreed.

Fezz grabbed his binoculars and stepped out onto the shoulder.

Khat pulled a black duffel bag out of the back seat and caught up as Fezz was stepping over the guardrail and moving into the wooded area just off the road.

Fifty feet in, the flat ground gave way to a steep slope. The tree line ended where the embankment started. Fezz and Khat stayed back a few feet to take advantage of the cover the trees and brush provided.

"Figures. It's pretty open," Fezz said.

Khat did not respond. He was busy comparing the physical building to the digital image he held in his hand.

The ground flattened out at the body of the embankment. There was a narrow grass strip and then a wide driveway, with diagonal parking spaces painted along its length. Beyond that was the long commercial building. There were doorways every fifty feet or so. A few of the doorways had signs mounted above them, but not all.

Fezz could see no activity below. There were three cars parked in adjacent spaces. A dark-colored Escalade, a silver SUV that Fezz guessed was an old Suburban, and a Cadillac sedan.

The driveway was lit by lamp posts, planted along the long drive-way. Fezz knew they would have no choice but to move through the lit area if they were going to get anywhere near the building.

"Look there," Khat said abruptly, "we've got movement."

A figure had emerged from one of the doors, located at about the midpoint of the building. Fezz did not have to use the binoculars he was holding. The light from the lampposts reflected off the white theatrical mask, and both Fezz and Khat knew what it meant.

"We're at the right place," Fezz said.

"I'd say that's an affirmative. We've gotta get in there now, Fezz. If it's not too late already, who knows how much time Mick's got."

Fezz lifted the binoculars and examined the costumed character.

"This one's armed," Fezz said. He dropped the binoculars.

"Alright. We need a workable plan. You realize we're going to have to go hot. You good with that, Fezz?"

"I was good with it before they had Mick. Now I'm looking forward to it."

Khat slapped his hands together as if they were cymbals. A wide beaming smile covered his face. "Hot damn, Fezz. How about this?" He started unpacking the duffel, pulling out a laptop and two pairs of EOTech night vision goggles. "We get close enough and we hijack the signal off the digital meter. If VEPCO can kill your electricity from their truck when you don't pay your bill, we can too. Not making any promises, but I can probably make it work. Where the hell is Mick when you need him?"

Fezz laughed, both at the dumb joke and at Khat's asinine plan.

"Why don't we just truck it down there and pull the meters by hand?" Fezz suggested.

Khat stared at him blankly. "Yeah. Or that," he said, cracking a smile.

"The lines come off the pole over there," Fezz said, pointing at the far-left side of the building. "The panel's going to be in that area."

Fezz lifted his binoculars and scanned the building again.

"There are cameras on four of the units, at least that I can see. There's no way we're getting in there without getting picked up by at least one of them."

They were going to be exposing themselves, no matter what they did. They already had been planning to take precautions, which would come in just as useful on the new, impromptu mission.

Along with thin body armor, Khat had packed balaclavas and tactical gloves. They were both wearing identical long sleeve Under Armour shirts, 5.11 cargo pants, and boots. Khat was confident that it would be impossible to visually identify them on the surveillance footage but was also aware that the exposure went beyond what the human eye could discern. Skilled investigators, with the right access and equipment, could run algorithms comparing body dimensions, gait characteristics, and movement patterns against huge databases of archived video. They would have to do their best to alter their natural movements while moving through the camera's field of view.

Khat reached into the bag to retrieve his weapon. He decided to leave his usual modified M4 rifle in the trunk, opting for a more inconspicuous Glock G17 9mm pistol. Fezz and Blake also frequently chose the Glock because of its proven reliability in the field. Like the others, Khat outfitted his G17 with an extended threaded barrel that allowed him to attach a suppressor. With the help of the subsonic ammunition, the Omega suppressor affixed to his 9mm pistol would dramatically reduce the chance of causing a scene.

There was also ballistics analysis to consider. Casings and projectiles would have telltale marks and striations that could later be matched with their firearms. Of course, they would not be holding on to the two pistols long enough for that to be a possibility. It would not be the first time that, following a mission, their team would have to disassemble their firearms and have the pieces melted down. Normally, the agency would take care of the "sanitation," as they typically called it. This time, they would need to figure something else out.

"All right let's get this show on the road," Fezz said.

Ritualistically, the two silently strapped on their body armor, checked their weapons and magazines, and slipped on the thick polyester balaclavas. They perched the night vision goggles on their foreheads, allowing easy access for when the time came.

They left the bag in the brush and began to move along the tree line. Fezz led and Khat followed, both with their eyes trained on the distant man in the mask.

Fezz stopped at a point where he felt they would have the straightest, smoothest shot at traversing the lit driveway toward the shadowy side of the building.

Fezz bent his knees and bounced lightly. He took a deep breath and watched intently. After several minutes, they could see the sole lookout start to move toward the steps. Fezz raised his hand, showing Khat the back of it. Khat began to bounce in rhythm.

The man walked up the two stairs, opened the door, and walked inside. Fezz kept his flattened hand raised up by his head. The man turned, looked back and forth down the length of the quiet driveway, and closed the door.

"Now," Fezz said as he began sprinting.

Khat followed, almost passing him before the two reached the left corner of the building. They pressed their backs to the brick exterior and caught their breath.

"I'll keep an eye out," Khat said, as he skulked to the corner and peered around toward the door of the unit they planned to assault.

Fezz looked at the row of electrical panels mounted to the building. There were six meters spinning, each making a faint buzzing noise. Each one was locked with a thin metal wire padlock installed, not so much to prevent access, but to detect tampering.

Fezz moved down the row of boxes, twisting the flimsy wire-locks until they broke free, and opening the door of each panel.

"We're both going to have to pull three, as fast as we can, then make a break for the door," Fezz said.

"Hold that thought, I've got movement," Khat interrupted.

"Roger," Fezz acknowledged.

Fezz and Khat held their positions. They each absorbed the mild exhilaration that comes in the quiet moments before the madness. For Fezz, Khat, and all the men who were built to exist in chaos, the air became fresher, time moved slower, and the quiet, still corner of the world became home.

"As soon as he steps foot back inside, we go," Fezz said.

The whirring sound of the traffic flowing along the nearby highway faded into the background. The two partners, bound by a promise to never leave a brother behind, stood cocked like the spring of the weapons they grasped.

28

Blake gasped as the cloth pulled away from his face. Like clockwork, the fat man immediately tried to engage him.

"Are you ready, or shall we try again?"

The real answer should have been "No. No, I would not like to try again." But Blake could not help himself. Irritating the fat man gave him his only solace.

"Try again," Blake said dryly.

For several moments, the fat man hovered motionless over him. Blake swore he could see a sour expression come over the stamped smile of the plastic mask, as if the fat man's frustration had begun melting it into a frown. He slowly walked toward the door and leaned in close to the ear of his goon posted on the right.

Blake realized he had made a mistake as soon as the snide comment flew out his mouth. The three had filled his head with water six times since he had woken up in the dank room. No normal person would be so cavalier. He had carefully feigned his distress up until that point, escalating his outward emotions appropriately.

Blake decided it was time to feed them a little information. To plant the seed that there was light at the end of the tunnel for them.

He knew, as well as anybody, that everybody has a boss. He considered it a good bet that these guys were getting worried about going back empty handed. Maybe, if he started getting chatty, they would not start second guessing their original assessment of him.

The fat man turned and began moving back toward the table.

"Okay. Look man. You don't need to try again. I really don't know much but I'll tell you what happened. Okay?"

The fat man glanced over at his men and then leaned against the table.

"Go on," he said.

"I was just messing around. I wanted to see if I could get in. I didn't see anything," Blake said.

He was intentionally vague. He had not accessed any system, but he knew that if these guys had something to hide, the fat man would fill in the blanks with his imagination.

"Rubbish," the fat man said. "We know what you found."

"I swear. I don't know."

The fat man motioned to his men. Blake exhaled with a slight sense of relief. He was familiar with that signal. It meant round seven. And round seven meant he had the fat man back on the hook. Blake started to consider how, if he played it right, he might be able to extract some information from the fat man before the night was over. He hoped he would be around to use it.

He saw the men begin to move, the one on the left stalked toward him with stretched-out cloth in hand. But the darkness came before the cold heavy cloth and its handler approached even halfway to him. The blackness was complete. A total absence of light in the windowless room.

Seize the moment.

Blake quickly bent his knees, flexed his abdominal muscles, and hoisted his upper body toward his feet. He clawed at the thick strap around his right ankle with both hands, trying to manipulate the buckle. He felt the metal table reverberate. A tinny twang rang out.

Blake figured the fat man had stomped the bottom of the table, expecting Blake's head to still be positioned there.

Blake freed the right strap and hooked the back of his knee over the back of the table to take the pressure off his burning abdomen. He went to work on the second buckle.

The voices of the silent men had filled the room. They called to each other in panic after the loud metal bang had echoed off the bare brick walls.

The fat man grunted, "Son of a bitch!"

Blake had pulled the slack through the loop on the left strap when he felt something brush against his right foot. Without hesitation, he cocked back his right leg and thrust it outward, letting the left strap support his weight. His foot connected hard with a solid fleshy mass.

The target let out a groan. Blake could not see a thing, but figured by the sound of it, that he had knocked the wind out of whoever he hit.

Blake released the strap around his left ankle and slid off the side of the table, opposite of the fat man. As he cleared the table, another loud crash echoed from the stainless steel. Blake slid underneath the table and swung his bound hands in an arc until he felt the legs of the fat man.

Before the interrogator could register Blake's current position, Blake had already balled up the bottom of one of the man's pant legs in his fists. He pulled swiftly and violently, leveraging the fat man's knee against the side of the sloping table. Tubs hit the ground, hard.

Blake slid his hand up the man's body, searching for his head. He pulled him closer to the underside of the table with every few inches he traversed. Blake and his adversary were each lying on their side, facing each other. They pawed and manipulated, each trying to get their bearings.

Blake tugged at the fat man's clothing to keep him from rolling out of reach and receding into the blackness.

The fat man swung his fist, connecting with Blake's shoulder and upper arm. Blake's arms were impeded by the thick metal table leg before he could reach the man's face.

Blake bent his elbows to move his hands around the table leg as a unit. He thrust his hands outward and felt the thin crinkly plastic of the mask.

The disoriented sentries continued calling out, no doubt trying desperately to locate and assist their leader.

Blake ran his hand under the mask, over the fat man's forehead, and toward the back of his head. Blake gritted his teeth as he yanked hard, using all his strength to send the fat man's forehead into the heavy metal table leg.

He reflexively grasped Blake's hands with his own, struggling to free himself from Blake's clamping grip.

He let out a scream as Blake slammed his head again and again. On the third time, Blake felt the rigidity of the man's skull soften. Instead of bouncing off the metal post with a twang, it sunk in quietly. Blake's abuser was dead.

"I will cut you," Blake heard a nervous voice yell out.

He figured that the remaining two men did not realize that the mortal combat they had witnessed with their ears had been occurring on the floor, halfway under the table. He visualized the pair staggering around the room like they were preparing to fight a ghost who preys on the living in the dark abyss.

Blake rolled onto the dead man's body and crawled back toward his feet. He hooked his bound hands under the man's feet and legs, working them toward the man's arm pits. Blake stood up, hoisting the man up in front of him. He pulled up quickly so that he could adjust his position and better support the limp, heavy body.

"Come get me," Blake taunted.

"Rob," one of the voices said. "Rob, you all right?"

Tubs' name is Rob? Really?

Blake labored as he dragged the dead man toward the sound of the voice. He called out to draw his enemy in. "Bad news boys. Rob's dead. Worse than that. You're next."

Blake felt a slight pressure as his cargo bumped into something directly in front of him. Blake felt the limp body pushing forcefully against him in a violent rhythm. The man behind the voice let out a guttural cry as he mustered the anger to repeatedly stab who he thought was the red-headed hacker who had been taunting him in the dark.

Blake made his move with perfect timing. He abruptly fell to his knees, letting the considerable weight of the corpse pull the handle of the knife from the assailant's hand.

Blake slid his hands down the front of the lifeless, crumpled human shield. He felt the handle of the knife, the blade buried deep into the ample gut of the dead man. He clutched the handle, pulled the blade from the flesh, and let the body slip through his arms to the floor.

"Did you get him?" the second, more high-pitched voice exclaimed.

"I think so," the other replied.

Blake sprang to his feet, wielding the knife in his right hand. He wrapped his left hand around the back of the right. He quietly moved toward the sound of the voices, swinging the knife back and forth in front of him, as if he were clearing a path through a dense rainforest. Each stroke was with the force that would be needed when he actually connected with his target.

"Stay down, unless you want to get stuck again," the deeper voice bluffed. He barely got the words out of his mouth when the six-inch blade sliced into the side of his neck.

Blake felt the resistance, but the momentum carried the blade through, only changing its original trajectory slightly.

Blake heard the man's body slap against the concrete floor. He felt a warm, slickness on the handle of the knife and gripped it tighter.

"One left," Blake goaded, "Come on over."

The remaining man did not answer.

Blake spun around, swiping at the darkness in wide, sweeping arcs. He wished that he could use the blade to cut his wrists free, but that would take some time and dexterity to pull off. He could not take the chance of getting caught off guard. Instead, he continued swiping at the air.

Blake heard a metal rattle and the sharp bang of the door flying open somewhere directly in front of him. A flash of light cut through the absolute darkness and Blake heard the distinct sound of the suppressed 9mm.

Fezz kept his infrared light trained on the man he had just shot. The man was slumped down in the corner to the left of the door. Fezz could see the large spray of blood on the wall behind where the man had been standing. He decided the man was dead. He surveyed the rest of his surroundings and saw the heavy man lying in a heap in the middle of the room. The damage to his face was catastrophic.

Fezz pointed his light toward Khat who was checking another man, lying in a pool of blood on the floor to the other side of the door. Khat and Fezz called out to Blake, who was still crouched, naked, and furiously swinging the large knife.

"Mick, it's us."

The sound of Fezz's voice immediately stopped the rapid flow of adrenaline that had been dumping into Blake's system. He stood up straight and let the knife slip out of his hand to the floor. The blade played a metallic melody as it bounced and settled onto the concrete. Blake let out a burst of laughter as he tried to calm his buzzing, overdriven nervous system.

"It's about time," Blake said.

Khat picked up the pair of jeans he found crumpled in the corner. He threw them at Blake, hitting him in the face.

"Put those on. For Christ's sake," Khat said.

Khat and Fezz scanned the hallway outside of the concrete room while Blake climbed into his pants.

They moved to Blake and stacked up. Fezz in front, Khat behind. Blake put his hands on Khat's shoulder. Khat pushed on Blake's back and, in turn, Blake pushed on Fezz. The three began to move toward the hallway with a choreographed gracefulness that had been ingrained over many years.

Blake relied on his sense of touch to follow. He moved his feet gingerly as the team picked up speed through the small facility.

Khat turned backward, keeping his back against Blake so that he could keep in physical contact while he covered the rear. He and Fezz had their weapons shouldered, scanning as they moved toward the exit.

"How many?" Blake asked.

"Six EKIA", Fezz responded. While they all commonly used the acronym for *Enemy Killed in Action*, Blake sensed that Fezz's response was more of a device that allowed him to avoid saying "We shot six people to death."

As they reached the exterior door, the weak light emitting from the streetlamps poured through the windows. Blake's eyes, adjusting to the darkness, began to resolve his surroundings. The three stepped over a body lying in the doorway. Blake noticed that the man was wearing a black hooded sweatshirt. A mask lay a foot from his body, next to the Uzi submachine gun he probably never had time to fire.

He looked at the man's face and noticed something peculiar. Something that struck him as significant. This man's face was pristine. Nothing like the burned, featureless soldiers that had invaded Anja's home and staged the dramatic assault on IPFG.

Khat pulled a balaclava over Blake's head before the three of them emerged into the brisk early morning air. Fezz and Khat pulled Blake across the driveway and up the embankment, toward the dark-blue sedan. Khat scooped up the duffel bag he had stashed as he passed.

Fezz jumped into the passenger seat while Khat moved around to the driver's side. He climbed in while tossing his night vision goggles onto the floor by Fezz's feet.

Blake hopped into the back seat and slumped back, out of view, as Khat began to drive.

Fezz twisted around and tossed a pocketknife onto Blake's lap. Blake went to work cutting his wrists free.

"Let's get you home, brother," Khat said.

"No. I have to finish this. There's still time."

Fezz tapped Khat on the leg. Khat glanced at him, then at the road, and then back at him. Fezz waited for a response to the unspoken question. The answer came with a simple nod. They were going.

"Text Griff," Khat suggested, "tell him we're back on."

"On it." Fezz said, only taking a few seconds to fire off the message. He tossed Blake's jacket to the back seat. "Here, you're going to need this. We don't want them mistaking us for a Chippendales telegram."

The three men shared a tense laugh as they drove, head-first, into battle.

29

Harrison pushed the earpiece into his ear. He twisted the knob, selecting channel eight. The front of his handheld radio read "SWAT." He pressed the button to transmit.

"Give us a heads up the minute it's clear. We'll be right behind you. If our guy is in there, no one talks to him until I get there," Harrison said.

Wells turned to Harrison. "So, you're giving the orders around here now?" A rare smile accompanied the reprimand.

"Sorry," Harrison said. He was aware that he became too excitable. He needed to maintain a level head. But he could barely contain himself, as he so badly wanted to get the man responsible for his partner's murder.

"Did you bring the copy of the search warrant?" Wells asked.

Harrison produced it from above the driver's side sun visor.

The two men waited. Harrison's leg bounced frenetically. Wells sat morbidly still.

"They're off," Wells said, directing Harrison's attention to the line of vehicles in front of them.

The lead truck pulled out, an armored MRAP vehicle that was

acquired from surplus Army inventory. The truck would provide cover for the deployment of the SWAT team, primarily riding in the second vehicle. The black SWAT personnel carrier, a glorified box truck, fell in behind the MRAP. An entire convoy of eight vehicles followed suit, with Harrison and Wells bringing up the rear.

Four minutes later, the convoy turned onto the dirt driveway toward the secluded old church. Hours of meetings and briefings all about this plan were about to be put into action. Harrison was giddy with anticipation. He stopped the car at the entrance to the driveway.

Harrison made sure he had a visual of the front of the building in the distance. He watched it intently as the team filed out of the truck and made their approach.

The crack of the flashbang reverberated through the air, possibly through the entire valley. Even though Harrison knew it was coming, he still jumped.

The team disappeared into the building, leaving only a few men to secure the perimeter. The radio fell into an eerie quiet for several minutes. Harrison suppressed the urge to key up and request a status update.

Finally, the commander's voice broke the silence. "All clear. Come on in, guys."

Harrison sped down the gravel driveway, jumped out, and made it to the door, all before Wells could get both feet out of the car. He pushed aside the splintered door and stepped inside.

The dilapidated structure was damp and had an overpowering earthy smell. Rubble was piled in the middle of the room. Scraps of soggy wood. Trash. The entire place was covered in green mold, empty beer cans, and bright-colored graffiti. Harrison did not need to see more. He already knew.

"Gotta be kidding!" Harrison yelled to no one in particular. "We screwed up."

30

Blake, Fezz, and Khat crouched down by the edge of the wood line, northeast of the structure. They could see only the right and front sides of the building. There were several windows along the side and, although many sections were boarded up, they could see the faint colors of the stained glass from the light shining through the panes.

"Someone's home," Khat said.

"Okay, I'll hike around the wood line and get a visual on the other side of the building. Khat can take the rear. At least we can make sure they don't have someone pulling guard duty on the perimeter. It would suck to have them coming at us from the rear too. Then we can converge in the middle and go," Fezz said.

"Hold up, Fezz," Blake interrupted. "Griff, are you still there?"

"I'm here," the tinny voice responded.

"Griff, do we need to clear the perimeter, or do you have a good enough view? I'd hate to waste the time hiking the loop if it's not necessary. Plus, I don't want us to take an unnecessary risk by separating if there are combatants lurking around out here," Blake suggested.

"I can give you better than that, gentlemen," Griff boasted. "I'm using thermal imaging. I can tell you for sure that, apart from a few little critters, you are the only living things out there. I can also tell you that there is most definitely heat being emitted from inside the building."

"Okay. Good. Look, there's no way to know how many, but I'd say there's a good chance whoever is in there is sleeping at this hour. My vote is we go now. Try to make a quiet entry, move through slowly until we can get a sense of what we're up against. If it goes loud, it goes loud. What do you think?" Blake's impatience was palpable.

"Yeah. I say let's just go. Let's get it over with," Khat said.

Fezz nodded in agreement.

"Okay. Griff we're heading in. I'm going to leave you on speaker with the volume up, so don't sneeze or anything. But do yell if you see anyone racing out that back door."

"Will do," Griff said.

"Okay, on me," Blake said as he left the concealment and sprinted toward the front doors of the church. Fezz and Khat followed.

They stacked up on the hefty double doors, Blake, then Fezz, then Khat. Each gripping an M4 Carbine in a low ready position. The rifles were each equipped with EOTech holographic sights and pressure-triggered lights. Fezz and Khat both used a vertical grip, mounted to the underside of the rail.

Blake's rifle, one of the backups Fezz had packed, was set up in a slightly different configuration than his own custom rig. The borrowed rifle was not equipped with a vertical grip or even a rail system. It did not matter, as he preferred to position his support hand tight against the magazine receiver in a more compact posture.

Blake gently pushed the rightmost door. It cracked open.

"It's open," Blake whispered. "See you on the other side boys."

Before every operation in the past decade, Blake would give the signal to go by saying "see you on the other side." He did not mean the afterlife, as his team originally thought, he meant the other side of the mayhem. The victory. He could not remember how it started but it had become a necessity. A superstition that, if skipped, would most definitely invite disaster. Blake had a sinking feeling that, no matter the talisman, disaster was inevitable.

Blake quietly pushed the door open another two feet. He leveled his weapon and the three slipped into the vestibule. There was a clear path from the door, but either side of the room was piled with wooden pews and other discarded pieces of furniture. The door directly in front of them was covered by heavy black drapes.

Blake reached the door and carefully poked at the center of the drapes with the muzzle of the rifle. He located the break, separating the two sections of curtains. He waited for the tap on his shoulder. When it came, he pushed through into the main hall of the church.

At every door, the team would enter the same way. The lead man would roll to the right, the next to the left while the third and fourth either covered the rear or headed up the middle, depending on if they were moving through the room or clearing the room and returning back the way they came.

But this is not what happened. Blake hardly made it two feet into the room before stopping cold. Fezz and Khat peeled off to either side of him and froze alongside Blake.

Six men in white plastic masks stood at attention in two lines of three, creating a path through the center of the nave. At the end of the path stood a single man. His face twisted with scars.

"Cosh," Blake said with certainty, still peering down the sights of his rifle, which were steadily trained between the man's eyes.

Fezz's rifle pointed toward the three men to the right. Khat covered the left. No one in the room moved an inch.

"I prefer Metus, if you don't mind Mr. Brier," he responded. His hands were folded in front of him. He wore no shirt or shoes. Only a pair of loose linen pants.

"I'm sure my men are happy to see you. They have been patiently waiting all night to welcome you."

Blake did not doubt that the soldiers had been standing at attention for hours. In fact, there was no amount of crazy that would surprise him when it came to Metus.

"I am unarmed. See." Metus slowly spun around in a complete circle. "Come Mr. Brier, let us sit down and talk. You are looking for answers. I have them. Come." Metus began to walk toward the arched doorway at the far corner of the room.

Blake shuffled forward several steps, keeping his sights in good position for a kill shot.

"Don't move," Blake ordered.

"Are you going to shoot an unarmed man in the back, Mr. Brier? I mean you no harm, come, let me show you something."

Metus moved to the archway and, with a methodically slow effort, crossed into the opening without looking back.

Blake darted to the archway and peered down the stone stairway. He could see that the stairs turned to the right in a rounded corner, plunging deeper into the ground. Flickering orange light reached out of the unseen space, rimming Metus's profile with a warm glow. The crooked field stone walls gave the scene a surreal, anachronistic quality. *If hell exists*, Blake thought, *it's probably at the bottom of these stairs*. Metus approached the corner, six steps down, and paused.

In the moment before Metus would slip out of view, Blake's mind churned through his options. As it was, Metus was a constant. If he let Metus slip out of his sight for even a second, he would become a variable. But was there an army waiting in the bowels, poised to mount an attack? If that were the plan, wouldn't they have done it already? They had the upper hand from the moment he entered, after all. And he did want answers. Aside from having Anja back, there was nothing he wanted more. There was no choice. He was obligated to follow.

Blake descended, following Metus around the corner. The bright holographic circle of his sights glued to the darkening figure.

Instinctively, Fezz and Khat moved through the human corridor, swinging their rifles back and forth between the rigid men. As they approached the archway, Fezz waved his hand, signaling Khat to follow Blake. Fezz took two steps down, just far enough to get some cover while maintaining the six men in his line of sight. He lowered himself onto one knee and supported his rifle on the other, a comfortable position that would give him a stable shooting platform and allow him to hold steady for a longer time.

At the bottom of the staircase, Blake entered the room. He was struck by the power of the atmosphere, as if the stones themselves were calling out from antiquity. A massive stone, laid across two uprights, formed an altar embellished with an ornate altar cloth, candles, chalices, and a brass incense censer. Carved pillars and flaming sconces rounded out the effect.

But Blake was not fooled. The archaic temple was nothing more than the stage of a deranged production, fashioned from an old crypt, or maybe a wine cellar. The dramatic manifestation of a sick mind. Metus was no prophet, no Knight Templar guarding the secrets of the old religion. He was not a supernatural force of evil, as he apparently fancied himself. He was just evil.

Hearing Khat reaching the bottom of the stairs, Blake looked over his shoulder, dropped his hand from the grip of the rifle and made a pushing motion. Khat received the message and maintained his position at the bottom of the staircase, just outside the temple room.

From Khat's current position, Blake figured, Khat could be at the side of either him or Fezz in seconds, depending upon the direction in which the situation started circling the drain. Blake hoped it was not both at once.

There were two chairs placed in the middle of the room, facing each other. Metus sat.

"Please, take a seat," Metus said. He held out his hand in a cordial gesture.

Blake kept his rifle trained on his adversary. He vowed to himself that he would not lower his weapon, no matter what happened, no matter what was said.

"I'll stand," Blake insisted. "Why don't you start enlightening me with all of these answers?"

"You haven't asked a question, Mr. Brier."

Blake had a million questions. But the one that rose to the top, that monopolized his mind during every waking moment, he was not ready to ask. Nor was he ready to hear the answer.

"What do you have against IPFG? What were you looking for? I know you were the CTO. Was it revenge? Did they have something to do with your accident?" The questions came to him in a wave and flew out of his mouth just as soon as they popped into his mind.

"That's a poorly formed question, Mr. Brier. But I'll do my best."

Blake wanted nothing more than to break the smug, condescending bastard into pieces. But that would not serve his purpose. Not yet.

"I admit," Metus started, "I do harbor some animosity toward the company. I know it is sinful, but I'm only human."

At least he acknowledges that much.

"After all, they did try to kill me. I mean, I'm sure he wouldn't admit it, but I have no doubt that Jacob Milburn and his little band of minions sabotaged my car to get rid of me. Silence me. See, I was getting suspicious. Milburn was giving outside contractors access to our systems, locking me out of certain facets of our infrastructure. I knew something was wrong and I said as much. It wasn't 'til after the wreck that I figured it out."

"Figured what out?"

"As I lay there, washed up on the rocky beach, a half mile from the wreck and a half inch from death, it dawned on me. Milburn was obsessed with the rising power of cryptocurrency. Constantly complaining that the board was not doing enough to stem the tide. The resurgence of a cash-type economy meant the bank couldn't take its cut. Couldn't manipulate the market. Like the board of directors, I was of the mind that we embrace the trends, figure out a way to support the emerging technology. Even contribute to its growth. That's what it was all about. What I stumbled onto without knowing."

"I don't follow," Blake said.

"Let me put it this way. I realized two things that day on the beach. The first being that Ray Cosh had to stay dead. There was no question about it. If they knew I was alive, they would almost certainly finish the job. And the second being, I realized that cryptocurrency was more than a fad, more than an experiment. It was a revolution, a chance to purify the greed and sin perpetrated by the financial industry. Everything happens for a reason, Mr. Brier. If I hadn't hit that water, I would surely be dead. Even still, it was an honest to God miracle that I survived. God's hand reached out and saved me. But why? The answer was simple. To give me the knowledge, Mr. Brier. To give me the power to lead a revolution."

Blake's inclination was to say something to the effect of "You're an absolute loon." Instead, he prodded further. "So, you got involved in the cause. The Cryptocurrency Evangelist Army. I get that. Sort of. But why the robbery. What was the purpose?"

"You don't get it, Mr. Brier. The future is at stake. We needed to act. Time is running out." Metus pulled a thumb drive from the pocket of his pants. "This is what we were after." Metus tossed the thumb drive in the air.

Blake released his support hand and snatched the memory stick out of the air.

"What's on it?" Blake asked.

"Before I tell you that, I have a question for you." Metus leaned forward in his chair. "Will you help me?"

Blake did not know whether to scream or to laugh. "Help you? And why would I do that?" He tried to keep his composure, to put the death of the woman he loved out of his mind, at least until he could get the answers he was looking for. But it was too much. He was no longer willing to play Metus's game.

"You sick man. You send your pathetic followers to kill an FBI agent. A woman I cared about deeply. And you ask me to help you? I'll kill you, you bastard."

Blake slid his finger onto the trigger. His entire body trembled.

"I did nothing of the sort, Mr. Brier. I sent those men to retrieve *you*. To recruit you to our cause. I wouldn't have harmed the woman.

You see, we have a mutual friend. Someone close to the cause, who seemed to think you would be a substantial asset to us. Let me ask you, have you received a sum of Bitcoin recently?"

Blake's mind reeled. He eased off the trigger and tried to process what he was hearing. Was it true? Were those men there for *him*? If so, would they have just taken him and let Anja be? He would make that trade in a second, but how could he have known? True or not, the mere suggestion plunged him into a bottomless pit of regret. How could he ever be sure that he was not responsible? He tried to save her, but, instead, he killed her. Just as sure as if he had pulled the trigger himself.

"You're lying," Blake said. His anger intensified. "I got a taste of your *hospitality* last night. Don't sit here and tell me that your men were not going to kill me after they finished torturing me. But that didn't turn out as you planned either, did it? Because all your so-called soldiers are dead, and yet here I stand."

"I don't know what you are referring to. I assure you, none of my men were involved in whatever happened to you last night. I told you, Mr. Brier, I am not your enemy. The enemy is Jacob Milburn. You must see that. Do you know why our friend converted your money into bitcoin? To prevent Milburn from having leverage. If your money were tied up in the banks, Milburn and his associates could erase your financial history, bankrupt you, just as he did me. But even he can't reach Bitcoin. Do you see the power? The freedom of cryptocurrency? We *saved* you." Metus shifted in his chair. "Okay. I will admit, I also hoped it would give you a little incentive. Give you some skin in the game, so to speak. But if you are as good as your reputation, you could make a difference. To the world. Do you believe in God, Mr. Brier?"

Blake had stopped listening. No longer able to process the words that were coming out of Metus's mouth, he retreated inside his own head, grappling with the gravity of the circumstances surrounding Anja's death.

"They came in with guns. They came to kill her," he said.

"No. I swear to you and to God. That was never my intention."

"You murderous asshole," Blake said. "God didn't save you. He deformed you so you would look as hideous on the outside as you are on the inside. You talk about saving people, about making things right. What about those people, murdered in cold blood during the robbery? What was their crime? Anja was an innocent soul. Did she deserve to die for your *cause?*"

"We are at war, Mr. Brier. The dead are merely casualties. They are of no consequence in the grand scheme of things."

The words echoed in Blake's head.

No consequence. NO CONSEQUENCE!

Blake darted forward and pressed the muzzle of his rifle against Metus's mangled forehead. Tears filled his eyes as his index finger pulsed on the trigger. He let out a pained, unintelligible yell.

"Don't do it," Khat shouted as he moved into the room. "It's not you, it's not what you're about. Mick. Mick, listen to me. Let's just walk out of here. We got what we came for."

"No. Khat. I didn't." Tears streamed down Blake's face. His skin was a crimson color, a physical presentation of the limitless rage that festered inside of him. "I promised her."

Metus sat completely still. His eyes closed; his posture relaxed. As if he were indifferent to death.

Blake pulled the slack out of the trigger. His conscience in an epic battle with his savage instinct. If he pulled the trigger, would he be just as bad as the soulless creature before him? He had spent his life fighting for the good guys, for freedom, for justice. He knew he could kill Metus with a flick of his finger, avenge Anja and the rest, but he could never go back. Everything he was, everything he believed in, would be wiped away in an instant.

"Blake," Khat said.

Blake registered Khat's voice, but it sounded muffled, as if they were underwater. Drifting apart in the inky blackness of the deep sea. He looked at Metus's face. Through the slack expression he saw the torment. Absorbed the betrayal. And then, without another word he mashed the trigger hard, sending a single 5.56mm round through Metus's skull.

As if in slow motion, he saw the spark as the projectile ricocheted off the stone at the far side of the room. He saw the brain matter fan out and speckle the floor. Ray Cosh may have died on that beach, years before. But it was Metus that would have to face his maker.

Blake breathed deeply, his chest expanding to its absolute capacity. He released the breath, and with it a piece of the burden he had been carrying. His next breath felt lighter, clearer. He did feel different, yes. But not in the way he had feared.

He *was* about justice. And justice had been served.

31

The deafening report reverberated off every stone, rushed through the archway, and broadcast its meaning through the small church. Instantly, the dormant soldiers broke free of their wooden postures and sprang for the edges of the space. Fezz scanned the room for the most immediate threat.

One of the men who had reached behind an olive colored cot propped up against the far wall spun around with a pistol in his hand. Fezz double tapped, dropping the combatant before he could fire a shot. He shifted his gaze to the other side of the room, just in time to see another soldier lifting a compact submachine gun. Fezz did not have time to address the new target. Instead, he threw himself into a prone position, pressing himself against the stone stairs.

Bullets whizzed by, landing high on the wall of the stairwell. Khat dove around the corner and crawled up the steps toward Fezz.

"I got one. Five more," Fezz said.

Blake rounded the corner and dropped to the ground. He worked his way upward and took a position behind Fezz and Khat.

"I guess that didn't go well," Fezz said, turning to Blake.

"As well as expected," Blake offered.

Khat brought his feet under him, leaning on the balls of his feet. "We need to spread out. Cover me."

Fezz switched the M4 to full auto and waited for a break in the barrage of bullets. "Go!"

As Fezz emptied the twenty-eight remaining rounds of the thirty-round magazine, Khat darted left out of the archway, rolled onto the riser, and dove behind the altar in the sanctuary. Fezz reloaded as Blake moved up to backfill Khat's position at the top of the stairs.

Blake peeked over the top step. One of the soldiers was moving toward the stairwell, pointing an AK-47. Blake ducked down, just before several more shots rang out. He did not hear the crack of the supersonic bullets passing overhead or their impact with the stone behind him. He peeked over the edge to see the soldier splayed out on the floor.

"Four," Khat shouted.

Another man, apparently following the last, retreated toward the vestibule. Blake lifted his rifle and fired. The soldier fell into the heavy black curtains, tearing down the entire rod on which they were fastened.

As the curtains landed in a heap on the dying man, two more soldiers were exposed, standing in the pathway that cut through the vestibule. They attempted to dive into the piles of junk on either side. Blake and Fezz fired, killing both before they could reach the cover.

Fezz called out to Khat. "One more."

"Roger," he acknowledged.

Khat sprinted the fifteen-foot distance between the altar and the lectern, which was perched on the edge of the riser to his left. No bullets chased him. He sat with his back to the wooden podium and pulled his legs in tight. He peeked around the edge of the lectern and scanned the side of the room closest to the stairwell. There, behind three hefty trunks, stacked one on top of the other, the shining toe of a boot protruded. The height of the three trunks together could not have been more than five feet tall, guaranteeing that the man hiding behind them was in a crouched position. Khat lined up his sights in the center of the middle trunk and squeezed off a round.

Blake saw the mask emerge from behind the stack of trunks in an arc toward the floor. The soldier hit the ground, rolled to his side, and began to push himself up with his right hand as he labored to lift the heavy AK-47 with his left. Blake, Fezz, and Khat fired simultaneously.

"That's all of them," Fezz announced.

Fezz, Blake, and Khat cautiously emerged and began clearing every crevice, checking that each of the combatants was truly deceased.

The three converged and moved through a rear door, situated on the opposite side of the church from the stairwell to hell. Beyond the door was a small sitting room and three more closed doors.

They grouped up to clear the room behind the furthest door. Fezz and Blake flooded the room, while Khat covered the other two doors. They cleared the bedroom, including the small closet and the space under the bed. They interpreted the setting, noting the religious artifacts and modern decor, and both agreed that the room must have belonged to Metus.

Working their way back toward the sanctuary, they hit the second door, which led outside.

They moved to the third door. Blake and Fezz burst in, each covering one side of the room. Even though the purpose of the procedure was to clear the building, Blake didn't expect to actually find someone. But find someone they had. A seriously injured man, sitting on a bed with his arms raised to his sides and his eyes closed.

"Don't move," Blake commanded.

Aaron Hosier opened his eyes. He stared into the barrel of Blake's rifle, then at him. "Is he dead?"

Blake nodded.

"Thank you," said Aaron, dropping his hands to the bed. "Are you the police?"

"No, we're not the police," Khat answered.

Aaron's eyes welled-up, he spoke only to Blake. "I think I'm dying, sir. Can you help me? I don't belong here."

A surge of pity washed over Blake. He could not imagine the pain the man must have endured. Open wounds oozed pus and his face was swollen in an absurd proportion to the rest of his body. His words were slurred and labored. Blake could tell the man's mental capacity was profoundly diminished. He assumed it was a result of sepsis or shock and not a preexisting condition, otherwise he would not have been recruited.

"What's your name?" Blake enunciated.

"Aaron, Aaron Hosier."

"Aaron," Fezz said, "listen to me. Your wounds are severely infected. You need a doctor immediately."

"Will you take me?" Aaron pleaded.

"I'm sorry, we can't, Blake said. "But hold on, I'll be right back."

Blake left the room and returned, moments later, holding a cellular phone.

"I saw it in the bedroom. Full battery," Blake said. "Aaron, I'm going to leave the phone on this table. As soon as we leave, you call 911. You understand?"

"Yes."

"And we would appreciate it if you never saw us, yeah? You heard the gun fire but hid in this room and never saw what happened. Can you do that for me, Aaron?" Blake said.

"Yes." Aaron paused. "If I don't make it, will you tell my mother I'm sorry?"

"You're going to make it," Blake said. "Just call 911, okay?"

With just his head, Blake made a motion toward the door. Fezz and Khat acknowledged with a nod and the three headed out. They used the rear door, then cut into the woods and blazed a two-mile long path back to where their vehicle was stashed, never slowing below a fast jog.

"Do you think he'll keep his mouth shut?" Khat asked, between quickened breaths.

"Not if he can remember talking to us, " Blake said. "But it was worth a shot."

All three kept their slung rifles pressed against their bodies to prevent the weapons from bouncing while they weaved and hopped over roots and rocks and fallen trees.

Khat let out a whoop. "Man! That was freakin' insane."

"Hell yeah it was," Fezz said. "How you feelin' Mick? Now that it's over."

"I'm good. But this isn't over just yet." Blake put his hand over the outside of his pants pocket and felt the contour of the thumb drive through the fabric. "Now I finish what Jo started."

32

J acob Milburn turned the Toyota Camry through the stone pillars framing the entrance to the long, cobblestone driveway. The four-cylinder motor screamed as he accelerated up the hill, toward the house. It had been so long since he drove a car, he forgot how exhilarating it could be. Although he owned several expensive sports cars, he rarely had time or occasion to drive any of them. His secretary's Toyota was far from a Ferrari, but that was exactly the point. He needed something average. Something that would not stand out.

Sheryl was elated when he told her he wanted to reward her hard work by not only giving her the rest of the day off, but by booking her a weekend stay at a spa resort. The gift came with a full spa package and the use of his personal driver. She wanted to kiss him when he told her he called ahead to Chanel for a stop at the boutique on her way to the spa. "Imagine the looks on the other women's faces," he had said to her, "when you step out of the Bentley on Monday morning, all done up, wearing a two-thousand-dollar outfit." To top it off, he told her to leave her keys so that her car could be detailed while she was gone. "The full executive experience," he called it.

In truth, Milburn was completely against showing any type of generosity, especially when it came to his employees. In his experience, it did nothing but embolden them. Make them feel entitled, less manageable. Like everything else in his life, he made an exception when it served his own agenda. And while, in hindsight, he probably could have dialed it back a bit and still gotten the same result, he was satisfied with how well the simple ruse had worked.

The driveway terminated in a loop that circled around a well-manicured patch of topiaries. Following the example of the other four cars that were already parked in front, Milburn traveled halfway around the circle, pulled to the right, and parked at the back of the line. He glanced at his watch. *Three minutes late.*

Milburn could feel his blood pressure rising. Normally, if he was fifteen minutes early, he considered himself late. But he had misjudged how long it would take to drive there. The roads he could once navigate in his sleep as a young commuter appeared strangely unfamiliar. If he had taken his phone with him, the turn-by-turn directions would have prevented him from taking the wrong exit and having to backtrack ten minutes. But Milburn was cognizant that even if he had not specifically called up directions, the mobile device would be tracking his movement. Creating a silent record of his journey.

As he approached the house, he was greeted by the butler, a slender man with an angular jaw and a rigid posture. He was ushered through the grand foyer to a set of mahogany doors. As his guide swung open the doors, the echoey expanse filled with the clamor of voices embroiled in debate. Milburn rushed in and took his place at the head of the long table. The chatter ground to a halt as the three men and two women registered his presence. All five sets of deadpan eyes settled on him.

Milburn cleared his throat.

"I assume you gentlemen, and ladies, have some concerns in light of recent events. Let me start by assuring you that I am handling it. I have been monitoring the numbers and, on our end, investor confidence has not taken a significant hit." Milburn chose his words carefully.

"Screw the confidence," said Arthur Benn III, "you've got the FBI poking around, for God's sake. This is going off the rails, isn't it?"

"Look Art, I understand your anxiety. But the FBI is a nonfactor." Milburn caught himself drying his sweaty palms against his legs. He hoped the others had not noticed and seen the cracks in his confident exterior. They were wolves in expensive clothing. If they sensed weakness, they would surely turn on him. And that was the last thing he needed. "The FBI is investigating a terrorist attack, not conducting an audit. We've given them no access to anything of substance."

"We've all got a lot on the line, Jacob," Gert said. A formidable presence and shrewd businesswoman, Gertrude Clark-Anderson was perfectly suited to be the CEO of the second largest bank in the United States. "We have one day to go, and *now* you want a meeting? I shouldn't even have agreed to host, you've probably brought the freakin' FBI to my doorstep."

"I promise, no one knows I'm here," Milburn said.

"Why are *we* here?" Gertrude fired back.

"We need to talk about a contingency plan." Milburn tried to explain, but his words were stepped on by the increasingly agitated Gertrude Clark-Anderson.

"Contingency! There is no contingency." With every word she spoke, Gertrude increased her volume in a linear crescendo.

"Let me spell it out again. If this doesn't go off, the stock doesn't spike, and the investors don't make the money they were promised. We do not get the performance bonuses that took three bloody years to negotiate. We're certainly not buying the controlling shares without it, which means..."

Gertrude tilted her head, keeping her eyes fixed on Milburn, her face filled with aggravation. He sat in defiance, refusing to answer the rhetorical question. He was aware of the consequences, including many that Gertrude probably had not even considered.

She continued. "Which means everyone in this room will be out of a job by Monday afternoon. So, tell me, Jacob. Tell me why you called this *contingency* meeting. And better yet, tell us all why you look like you've been on a three-day coke binge."

Milburn considered telling her, all of them, the truth. That Cosh's plan had worked. That he was in possession of enough information to burn it all down. To bury IPFG. To bury him. Or should he tell them that, despite years of planning, some red-headed guttersnipe showed up out of the blue, threatening everything they had worked towards?

He wondered what they would say if he told them why he looked like warm garbage. That it was not the FBI that kept him from getting an ounce of sleep, it was Blake Brier. The people who were supposed to neutralize Brier had military experience. Training. What chance did he have when Brier came for him? He had made a mistake, something he rarely admitted. He underestimated the man and feared that his error had put his life in jeopardy.

"That's why I love you Gert, you tell it like it is," Milburn said, forcing a positive tone, along with a smile. "All I am saying is that we need to be on the same page if something goes wrong. If, after the fact, the software does not successfully wipe all traces of itself, for example. If there was evidence still out there."

"Let's say that happened," Edward Brant chimed in. "Couldn't it be blamed on this CEA group? The whole country has seen the coverage at this point. It wouldn't take much to spin a narrative that they were behind it. We got lucky with them pulling that stunt. Isn't that the smartest play?"

"Yes. I agree. But I mean, what if we have to flee or go into hiding?" Jacob asked.

"Hiding? I'm not going into hiding. You said this couldn't come back on us." Erin Stadelnik's voice was sweet. Milburn could never understand how she could command a company of any substantial size. But she had done so.

Paul Lockland, who headed the smallest of the institutions represented at the table, spoke up. "When you hired these people, you swore up and down they were the best. That after it was done, there would be no trace. So why isn't Robert here? The whole purpose of spending that much money was so he and his people would take care of the dirty work, like they did with Ray Cosh. You tell Robert, any issues that arise are his problem and we expect him to handle it. Or put me in touch with him, I'll tell him myself."

Like they did with Ray Cosh. Exactly.

In the beginning, Milburn was skeptical that the plan could even work. But Robert had made a strong case. It seemed sound, foolproof even. And when Cosh began to catch on, it was taken care of swiftly. Milburn remembered thinking to himself that the exorbitant fee was money well spent.

In retrospect, what did Robert and his men truly accomplish? They failed to take Ray Cosh out of the equation. In fact, the problem was made exponentially worse.

And what about Blake Brier? He failed there too. All he did was get himself killed. Robert made a million promises but, in the end, was not able to keep any of them.

Milburn could not bring himself to tell the people in the room that they had all been ripped off. He had made promises too. It was a reflection on him.

"Robert no longer works for me," Milburn said.

"You fired him? This late in the game? Why would you do that?" Brant's hot-headed nature began to show.

"He became inefficient," Milburn said.

"You know what, why don't you do your job, Jacob," Gertrude said. "We have all done our part. We brought in the money, we structured the mergers, we went to bat with our respective boards of directors to set up the necessary deals with IPFG. Your only job was to make sure the technical side was taken care of. I swear to God, Jacob, if you screw this up, you're not taking me down with you. You've wasted everyone's time here. Goodnight, Oscar will see you all out."

Gertrude stormed out of the room. The rest of the attendees got up and trickled toward the door. Milburn stayed seated.

Arthur Benn stopped and placed his hand on Milburn's shoulder. "You've got to pull yourself together Jacob. You really do look a mess. Just one more day. Hang in there." Then, he left.

Milburn sat at the head of the table, head in hands. Alone.

33

B lake fired up a virtual machine, inserted the thumb drive, and copied its contents onto the machine.

"Whatever this is, there's a ton of data," Blake said, waiting for the copying process to finish. When it finally completed, he passed the thumb drive to Griff, who had set his laptop at the end of Blake's desk.

"Throw me that stick when you're done," Khat said, pulling a chair to the other end of the desk. "Uh, Mick, do you have another laptop I can use?"

"In the cabinet," Blake said.

Khat plucked one of several thin laptops from the metal cabinet and rejoined the others. He went to work setting up the machine.

"Oh, yeah, the case is as good as solved, now that Khat's on it," Fezz jabbed.

"Hey, I may not be as good as these two geniuses, but I can hold my own."

"I'll have to give you that, Khat," Blake said. "Only because I taught you everything you know."

"Just give me the stick." Khat yanked it from Griff's hand.

"Seriously Khat, the more eyes the better. Let's see what we've got here." Blake opened the copied folder in a code editor. The language-aware software intelligently colored textual code to make it easier to read.

Blake browsed through the files. "Well, it's JavaScript, I can tell you that much. Some kind of web client software."

"Do you have any beer in your fridge?" Fezz asked.

"Yeah, grab me one too," Blake said.

"I'll take one," Khat added.

"Make it a full round, barkeep," Griff said.

"I see you're fitting right in, Griff," Fezz said as he left the room and bounded up the stairs.

"Looks like this is the production code, it's been minified and uglified. We're going to have to reformat this first to make heads or tails," Khat said.

"We're a step ahead of you, bud," Blake said. "I'm looking at basic authentication handling here, some http communication services. I think this is their standard online banking client, which does not make sense. The size of the sum of these files is way too big to deploy over the web. Maybe there's a couple of years' worth of backups on here."

"I agree," Griff said, "but it's definitely a banking client, look at the main routine. The first method called loads modules based on the access URL. See the module file names? IPFG, United Bank, Midwestern. There's dozens of them. These are big banks. Are they really outsourcing their online platforms to IPFG?"

"That *is* peculiar," Blake agreed.

"What am I looking at here?" Khat turned his screen toward Blake. "There's some cryptographic stuff here, this section's doing some hashing right?"

"What's the name of that file?" Blake said.

"Service-worker.js," Khat responded.

Blake and Griff both brought up the file on their machines.

"So, a typical service worker runs in the background, in the browser. It usually handles caching and push notifications for progressive web apps," Blake explained.

"Holy crap!" Griff slapped the table. "Khat's right. The service worker is doing cryptographic work. Look here, this line is comparing hashes, this thing is looking for a nonce. This is mining software. How much you want to bet it's mining Bitcoin?"

"Wait a minute, IPFG is mining Bitcoin?" Blake thought out loud. "Is that what this has all been about? I mean, between all the banks, there must be millions of users. So, I guess, even though the browser is not going to have access to the hardware level, when you put millions of slower processes together, you'd still have a pretty powerful mining network. And the customers would have no idea they're participating."

"This should have been noticed already," Griff said. "A network like this should be mining most of the blocks on the blockchain. They'd be pulling in millions of dollars."

"Unless," Blake paused. He sorted the subfolders by size. One stood out as being incredibly large. He opened the folder and looked at its contents. "Look at this: .dat files, index, chain state. This is the blockchain."

"So? That would make sense, wouldn't it?" Khat asked.

Fezz entered, carrying four tall yellow cans. "I love this stuff. Man, do they know how to make a badass beer in Vermont!" He traveled around the desk, passing out the cans.

"You are just in time, my friend," Blake said, accepting the cold can. "I think I know what's going on here. They're not mining Bitcoin. Not exactly. Griff, download the current blockchain. We're going to have to do some comparisons."

As Fezz looked on, Khat and Griff prepared the necessary software to comb through the two chains, block by block. The one obtained by the CEA from the IPFG servers, and the one downloaded from the official public source. They worked backwards, starting at the newest common block. None of them drank even half of their beer before the pattern became evident. Even to Fezz.

"I knew it. It's a fifty-one–percent attack," Blake exclaimed. "They've been maintaining a separate blockchain. It makes perfect sense now. The robbery, Milburn's evasiveness, all of it. You saw that in the IPFG version of the blockchain, all the transaction amounts are changed to one-millionth of a Bitcoin, the smallest possible transaction. At least as far back as you looked. Which means that each altered block had to be mined. That's where the banking client comes in."

"But what good does it do to maintain a separate blockchain?" Khat asked.

Griff jumped in. His excitement was infused into every word. "Because if you can keep the fake chain as long or longer than the legitimate one, at some point you can swap them out."

"If," Blake interjected, "you control at least fifty-one percent of the network." Blake pushed his screen toward Fezz and Khat. "While you guys were comparing, I went through the rest of the code. It's beautifully simple. The client receives a block and a range of nonces to try. It reports back if it successfully mines the block. The code itself is just doing simple calculations. It wouldn't be noticed unless you were looking for it."

"Okay, so millions of computers are working on the same block at the same time, using a different set of random numbers so they don't duplicate work. Right?" Fezz said.

"Exactly. And I'd bet IPFG has a massive amount of computing power devoted to it as well. The concept is used all the time by mining pools. Participants sign up to contribute processing power and get some fraction of the block reward when the pool is successful. In this case, the participants don't get a dime. They don't even know they're part of a pool. IPFG retains all the mined coin, which will be legitimate once the chains are swapped. All the Bitcoin earned by actual mining firms would be wiped out."

"It's ingenious. All you need is enough people to visit your website on a regular basis. That's why IPFG is hosting the online banking software for all those other banks," Griff said.

Fezz blurted his own epiphany, "Those other banks must be in on it too."

Griff nodded. "Without a doubt."

"With all of this in place, why hasn't the real blockchain already been affected?" Khat looked to Griff and then to Blake for an answer.

"The blockchain grows every ten minutes. It could take years to catch up, even if you have more processing power than most of the network. It seems like they did the math, the timeline is hardcoded. See this section here." Blake pointed out the relevant block of Java-Script code. "Milburn's cluster joins the real network tomorrow morning. We have until then before it's pushed out."

"The IPFG version of the chain was copied almost a week ago. It was probably just about the same length as the legitimate one at that time. By now, I'd bet it's ahead," Khat said.

"Are we losing you, Fezz?" Griff asked, evidently noticing Fezz's blank expression. "Is it clear why that matters? Since the false chain will be the longest chain *and* because most of the network, controlled by Milburn, will verify the new chain as the legitimate one, the doctored blockchain will replace the legitimate one. Forever. You guys understand what that means, right?"

"It means Milburn will be richer than he already is," Fezz said.

"No. It means that anyone who spent Bitcoin, for who knows how long, can re-spend the same coin, because the history would be permanently changed. The network would continue building on the false chain, solidifying it, irreversibly," Griff explained.

"In which case, Bitcoin would essentially be worth nothing," Khat said.

Blake hopped out of his chair. "Yes. Not only Bitcoin, but all cryptocurrency would be suspect. The demonstration of the vulnerability would essentially kill cryptocurrency. It would bankrupt its users and drive everyone back to the banks."

"So Metus was actually trying to save Bitcoin. He may have been right. Milburn probably did try to have him killed when he started noticing that something was up," Khat said.

"That's likely," Blake said, "but he took it too far. He could have gone to the authorities. He could have done any number of reasonable things. Instead, he murdered innocent people."

"I'm not justifying his actions, just remarking that he wasn't lying about Milburn," Khat clarified.

"So how do we stop this?" Fezz asked.

"We have to rewrite the software to neutralize it. But we'll need to deploy it to every customer before it's triggered," Blake said.

"In order to do that, we'll need to gain access to IPFG's systems. Just as the CEA did," Griff suggested.

"Well we're certainly not staging a robbery, Griff, if that's what you mean." Fezz's demeanor took on a serious undertone.

"That won't be necessary," Blake said. "I have another idea."

34

Blake got off the elevator on the twelfth floor. A stark contrast to the bustling ground floor, the area featured a more quiet, swank atmosphere. Plush couches and potted plants filled the open expanse in front of him. Two men in expensive suits, legs crossed, sat engrossed in stacks of paper, printed in colorful ink.

Dressed in a Brooks Brothers suit with a salmon-colored tie and matching square breast pocket, Blake blended in. As he moved about the building, his presence had not garnered a second look. He approached the two men.

"I'm here to see Mr. Milburn, would you mind directing me to his office?" Blake said.

"Get in line," one of the men said. The other chuckled.

"Are you from accounting?" Blake said.

"Marketing," one of the men replied. "And you are?"

"The name's Shea, I'm with the SEC," Blake replied.

"Oh, my apologies," the younger man said. "End of the hall on the right." He pointed out the direction.

"Much obliged," Blake said, heading off toward the wide hallway.

He approached the double doors, conveniently marked with a

placard that read "Jacob Milburn, CEO." Blake straightened his tie and entered.

"Can I help you?" A smartly dressed woman said from behind a high counter that bordered her L-shaped desk.

"You must be Sheryl," Blake said.

"Yes, that's right, and you are?" Sheryl inquired.

"Jacob is expecting me." Blake barreled through the reception area, throwing open a second set of double doors.

"You can't just--" Sheryl started, in protest. But Blake had already disappeared into Jacob Milburn's office.

Jacob Milburn sat at his desk, the receiver of his phone to his ear. Blake sat in one of two leather-upholstered chairs, positioned directly in front of Milburn's desk. The look on Milburn's face was one of complete surprise, if not terror.

Milburn took the phone away from his ear but still spoke into the handset. "I've gotta go," he said, and hung up the phone.

"What do you want from me?" Milburn asked. His voice wavered. Blake almost did not recognize him as the same man he had spoken to only two days before. The confidence, no, the hubris, gone, replaced by a crazed anxiety.

"I just want to have a conversation, Mr. Milburn, nothing more," Blake said.

"Are you here to kill me?"

"Kill you?" Blake laughed. "Oh, I see, you're worried that I took offense to you sending your mercenaries to torture and kill me. Is that it? Water under the bridge, Jacob. Can I call you Jacob?"

"Sure," Milburn said. He most certainly was not going to say no. "About that."

"Forget it. Like I said, water under the bridge. What I really want to talk to you about is investment opportunities. I've got some cash to spend, see, and I hear you're the guy to talk to about making some wise investments."

Milburn perked up. The apprehension began to melt away from his face. Just as Blake predicted, the fear of violent retribution began to subside, giving way to the arrogance, lying dormant beneath. Milburn did not understand motives of loyalty or righteousness. But he was well acquainted with the motive of money. All the wickedness in his world was driven by it.

"Cash? Mr. Brier, I'm sure you're not serious. I don't know what you may own in stocks but I'm pretty sure you don't have much in the way of liquid assets. You don't even have a checking account, do you Mr. Brier?"

"No, you're right. I don't. You've done your homework. I expected that. The thing is, I'm pretty heavy in Bitcoin. Are you familiar with Bitcoin?"

"A bit," Milburn lied.

"Let me tell you a story about Bitcoin," Blake said.

Milburn squirmed in his seat at the mention of the word. Blake reveled in his discomfort. If Blake were Jacob Milburn, he would be thinking about how to summon his secretary, or anyone, without offending the dangerous lunatic sitting in front of him.

"Once there was a man who ran a bank," Blake continued. "It was a big bank that controlled a lot of money. But he wasn't satisfied with that, because this cryptocurrency started gaining popularity. Started trading at astronomical prices. The man, let's call him Jacob, started thinking that there must be a way to leverage all of his power to kill this trend, to undermine it. He was a smart man, you understand? A real innovator. He had devised a way to exploit the technology that would surely kill it. He enlisted the help of other powerful people, the heads of other large banks. And it was foolproof. Except he had enemies. Enemies of his own creation."

"I've heard enough, Mr. Brier," Milburn said.

"I'm not finished," Blake snarled. "What this bank executive didn't count on was that a woman, an FBI agent, had his number. She knew he was shady. And she set in motion a chain of events that would take him down."

"Enough of this," Milburn said. "If you've come to kill me, do it already. Otherwise, get out of my office. I get it, you've worked it all out. Except you have no proof and you never will. The thing is, in a few minutes, it will all be done, and there's nothing you can do about it."

"Well, that's where you're wrong, Jacob. It is already done, just not the way you expected. You see, overnight, I replaced your software. Rendered it useless to your purpose. At least half of your users will be logging in this morning and inadvertently updating the service workers with the new version. In thirty minutes, when the timer hits zero, you won't have fifty-one percent." Blake sat back in the chair. "Isn't that a bitch?"

"Not possible. You would need access to our systems. I spared no expense in security. It's just not possible."

"You're right. I mean, the security surrounding customer data is abysmal. You probably should have been making that your priority, huh? But the servers hosting the web client, top notch. Really impressive. You'd have to get physical access. And Ray Cosh knew that, didn't he? Luckily, I had a little help."

Milburn sat dumbfounded, as if watching an opera being performed in a language he could not understand.

"Steve. Come on in," Blake said.

The door opened and Steven Reid appeared, a satisfied smile on his face.

"Jacob, this is Steven Reid. Do you remember him?" Blake asked.

"No. Who is this?"

"This is the man you fired to protect your little secret. Ring a bell? Last night I gave Steve a call. And as it turns out, he was more than happy to help. The best part, you're going to love this, his access key fob was never deactivated. That was a hell of an oversight on your end, right? Any who, once we had physical access, it was trivial to upload the modified version of the client software to the servers."

"You imbecile!" Milburn cried. "Do you know what you've done?"

"Oh, we're pretty sure, yeah. We've gone and screwed up your plans pretty good." Blake said.

"You screwed yourself, Mr. Brier. You are a murderer. You killed my associates. You're threatening my life. I've been working with the FBI, you know, all I have to do is make a call and you're finished." Milburn said.

"No need, Jacob," Blake said. "You can tell them in person."

Blake paused, waiting for the big entrance. The grand reveal. After contacting Reid, Blake reached out to Andrew Harrison and told him everything. Well, a lot of it. He told Harrison about his relationship with Anja and the events that led up to her murder. He filled in the backstory about Ray Cosh's assassination attempt and the birth of the CEA. And most importantly, he explained Milburn's plot and his own plan to stop it. Together, they came up with the idea of wiring Blake with a microphone and sending him into Milburn's office.

In a visual display of his mental process, Milburn's expression morphed from confusion to dejection.

There you go, Jacob. Now you get it.

Finally, the door opened, and Harrison stepped into the room.

"Jacob Milburn, you are under arrest," Harrison said. Blake basked in Harrison's obvious joy as he applied handcuffs to Milburn's wrists.

Justice.

"You are making a mistake, Agent Harrison. These men are working with the CEA. They planted software on our systems. You should be arresting them."

Harrison pulled Milburn close. "This morning I had a little meeting with a Gertrude Clark-Anderson. Lovely lady. You wouldn't believe how quickly she took the offer. Full immunity if she steps down from her position and testifies against you and the others. She was quite detailed, Mr. Milburn. Dates, times, names. I don't know how someone is that organized. I guess that's how she became so successful, eh?"

The color drained from Milburn's skin. He lowered his eyes to the floor and avoided any further eye contact with Blake or Reid as Harrison escorted him out of the office.

In a way, Blake understood the relief that Milburn must have felt. Considering the circumstances, there was no longer a need to propagate the lie. To wear the mask. Blake had experienced the same feeling when he reconnected with Anja. Revealed his own past. The freedom of being able to own the truth was liberating.

"Thank you, Steve," Blake said, with a handshake.

"Very glad to help."

"So, are you back on the clock?" Blake asked.

"Not officially until tomorrow. The board met this morning and already appointed Mills as interim CEO. Not only did he agree to rehire me, but he gave me a promotion. I'm actually going downstairs to fill out the paperwork after this."

"That's fantastic. Jo, Agent Kohler, would be glad to know that. She wanted to make it right."

"You know it wasn't her fault, right?"

"Yeah, I know. Still. I'm glad it worked out," Blake opened the door. "Take care, Steve."

Blake called the elevator and turned back toward Sheryl Pannikin. "May I say, you look stunning."

Sheryl's face reddened, "Thank you."

Blake stepped into the elevator. "Oh, and I love the Bentley."

35

Blake shifted his weight. The soles of his polished Oxfords dug further into the soft, mossy ground. Residual droplets, left on the leaves of the sycamore by a brief morning rain, trickled down on him. Hardly able to recall what it felt like to sleep, he leaned against the sturdy trunk.

A hundred feet away, a few dozen people huddled in a loose circle, each clutching a single white rose that contrasted with their obligatory black clothing. A thin fog gave the entire scene a surreal quality. A nightmarish painting, immortalizing a twist of fate that upset the balance of true justice in the world.

Blake swallowed hard. He could feel the lump of grief and guilt sink to his stomach. But it was not the guilt that kept him lurking in the shadows. It was longing. When he was with Anja, when he felt her body pressed against his, he felt like they were the only two people in the world. He needed his goodbye to share the same intimacy. Just her. Just him. One last time.

Blake was relieved that Anja's family had arranged for the private burial ceremony. Earlier that morning, the public funeral held at St. John's Church drew an enormous crowd. Hundreds of federal agents, politicians, and average citizens showed up to pay their respects. With the small church quickly filling to capacity, many gathered in Lafayette Square, standing vigil with candles as they watched live coverage on their cell phones.

Blake had to hand it to the FBI and the federal government. They could not have done more to honor Anja's life and career. The ceremony included full military-style honors and a poignant speech by the director himself. She deserved every bit of it and more. But Blake could not help but think that Anja would have disapproved of the scale. Especially the media circus that accompanied it.

It eased his heart to know that, in the end, she would be sent off into eternity in a setting of modesty and tranquility.

From where he stood, Blake could hear the words of the priest. He could sense the agony of the friends and family that gathered around the ornate white casket as it was lowered into the muddy ground. He took solace in knowing that their grief would one day subside, eventually giving way to warm memories. But he was not sure it would be the same for him. He could not imagine a path that would lead beyond the guilt. He had no doubt that it would haunt him for the rest of his life.

Tears welled in his eyes as he watched the crowd thin. One by one, each approached the gaping hole in the earth and tossed a rose on top of Anja's casket. Each had lingered in silence for varying amounts of time before turning away and walking off to their cars. Blake wondered what they had said to themselves in those fleeting moments. Had they spoken to their God? Had they spoken to Anja? What did they say to her? What would he have said?

Blake watched as Fezz, Khat, and Griff stepped toward the grave. They paid their respects and then somberly walked past the few remaining people. Fezz glanced over at Blake and tapped his fist on his chest. Blake nodded. The simple gesture spoke volumes. Fezz understood. All three of them did. And they would be there when he needed them.

In the end, only one person remained. Kneeling at the edge of the grave, Harrison clutched his rose. Blake could feel his hesitation, his fear that saying goodbye would somehow make it more real.

People often say they wish there was something they could do. Seeing Harrison's grief, he realized there was something he could do. He knew what Harrison needed. And, for Anja, he would give it to him.

Blake left the cover of the sycamore and weaved through the stone markers until he stood beside Harrison. Neither said a word for the better part of a minute.

"I..." Harrison started, but fell silent again.

"I know." Blake said, placing his hand on Harrison's shoulder.

"I never got to tell her."

"You didn't have to. She already knew," Blake said. "You didn't miss your opportunity to tell her how you felt about her, you showed her every day. She cared for you deeply. Not just as a partner, but as a person. She loved you, I could tell by the way she talked about you. And I know she'd want you to know that."

Harrison smiled, put his hands over his face and sobbed.

"Thank you," Harrison said, pulling himself together. "Thank you."

Harrison opened his hand and let the flower fall onto the pile that had accumulated on top of the casket. He stood up, brushed off his knees and extended his hand. Blake did the same.

"Day after tomorrow?" Harrison said.

"I'll be there," Blake replied.

Harrison smiled and walked off.

Blake exhaled loudly.

ANJA JOHANNA KOHLER. The letters, carved into the solid granite headstone, seemed like a mistake. Letters that should not have been arranged in that particular order, in this particular place. Not yet. But there they were, etched forever in history.

"I was thinking about what I would say to you if you could hear me. I wanted to say I love you, but you already know that. That I miss you. That I regret the time we lost, the time we could have been together if I hadn't pushed you away. But you know all of that, too. What you don't know, what you'll never know, is how sorry I am that this happened to you. That I caused it to happen to you."

Tears streamed down Blake's cheeks and dripped from his beard.

"So that's it. That's what I am going to say."

Blake cleared his throat and wiped the moisture from under his eyes.

"I'm sorry, Jo. I'm sorry."

36

"How long did you sleep?" Fezz asked.

"Eighteen hours straight, no lie," Blake said.

Khat flagged the bartender. "Can we get another round? Thanks."

"Yeah," Griff said. "You were pretty useless cleaning up the church, I think you fell asleep standing up at one point."

Blake shrugged. "What can I say boys, I had a rough week."

"What are you complaining about? I did all the heavy lifting. How many holes did you dig, Griff?" Fezz said.

"I still can't believe that kid didn't call 911," Khat said. "I mean, even though it did kind of work out better for us. There would have been a hell of a lot of hoopla when the ambulance showed up and found seven faceless corpses. Still, he probably would have lived if he had just called."

"Aaron Hosier. That's what he said his name was," Blake said. "I plan to find his mother. He asked me to tell her he was sorry. So, I'm going to."

"You're a stand-up guy, Mick," Fezz said. "No matter what Khat says about you."

Fezz mushed his meaty palm into Khat's face. Khat swatted it away.

"The only crap I talk is about you, ya big ogre," Khat said.

"I really appreciate you guys having my back. I owe you big. All of you," Blake said.

"Especially Fezz." Khat smiled at his own joke before he even started it. "Didn't you know he single-handedly fought off thirty-eight of those Evangelist guys, armed only with a spoon?"

Fezz played along. "Come on, it was only, like thirty, at the most."

"All I know is, next time, I'm coming along," Griff insisted.

"Let's hope there isn't a next time," Blake said.

"What? Now that you're back in the swing of things, aren't you coming back to the team?" Fezz asked, only half-jokingly. "We could use you. The more geniuses the better, right?"

"I'm not sure what I'm going to do now that I'm between jobs again. I think I'm going to travel a bit. Get my head straight. We'll see. The first thing I've got to do is open a bank account and start moving some cash into it." Blake said.

The bartender, a cute blonde wearing a midriff shirt that showed off her belly ring, set the four bottles on the bar in front of the group. She peeled a cocktail napkin off the stack and jotted a phone number. She placed one of the beers on the napkin and slid it to Blake. "On the house," she said.

"How? Seriously, how?" Khat howled. "Every time."

"Two words. Animal. Magnetism." Blake grinned.

They each scooped up a bottle. Fezz raised his in the air. The rest followed.

"To Anja," Fezz said.

"To Anja," the group repeated.

"So, Harrison turned out to be a pretty cool guy? How'd you leave it with him?" Khat asked.

"I have to meet with him tomorrow to give my formal written statement about that night at Anja's. He didn't push too hard about the rest of it. He's never heard your names, if that's what you mean," Blake said.

"No, just wondering. Lately we've had a couple of issues where we had to work in conjunction with the FBI. Wasn't a great experience. It'd be nice to have a contact who's trustworthy. Someone who's decent, that we don't mind working with," Khat said.

"I'd say he'd be a good candidate," Blake said. "Jo trusted him."

"Hey," Griff interrupted. He pointed at a TV screen mounted high behind the bar. "Look at that, is that about Milburn?"

The subtitle of the Fox News commentary read, "Bitcoin Bombshell."

"Excuse me," Fezz asked the bartender, "would you turn the sound up for a second?"

She grabbed the remote and caught the anchor mid-sentence.

"—experienced a shock. A Nakamoto fan club has long been monitoring Bitcoin addresses, believed to belong to Satoshi Nakamoto himself, hoping to catch any activity. Last week, they say, they found just that. Around two hundred thousand dollars' worth of Bitcoin was spent from several addresses that contained Bitcoin mined in the first few blocks of the Blockchain. Absolute proof, experts say, that Satoshi Nakamoto is alive. Here to explain is Technical Correspondent Murray Inusan."

"Okay, you can turn it down. Thank you," Fezz said. "Nope, not about Milburn."

"Too weird to be a coincidence though, right?" Khat said. "Nakamoto resurfaces just as all of this is going down?"

"Coincidence or not, he definitely wanted it to be noticed," Griff said. "Of all the possible addresses that are believed to be associated with Nakamoto, using coins mined in the first few blocks ensures that it would be linked to him. It couldn't be anyone else. He had just invented it at that point."

"I wonder what he bought," said Fezz.

"Wait a minute," Griff said, lifting his palm as if trying to stop traffic. "It's not a coincidence. Not at all. Blake, do you have the original addresses from when you were sent the Bitcoin?"

"It's in my transaction history on my wallet app. But there's no way."

"Just look it up and read one off to me." Griff took out his phone and navigated to an online Blockchain explorer.

Blake humored him. He called up the info and started reading off the chain of letters and numbers, "1HLo D9E4 SDFF PDiY fNYn kBLQ 85Y5 1J3Z b1"

"Okay, let's see," Griff said. "The first transaction for this address was on January 9, 2009. Fifty Bitcoin mined at block number two! That's essentially the first Bitcoin ever. The first block isn't spendable. Holy crap, Blake. This is incredible. And you communicated with him."

"No way," Blake said, snatching the phone from Griff's hands. He studied the information, clicking from block to transaction to address and back again.

"Well, I definitely didn't see that coming," Fezz said. He called out to the bartender, "One more round."

Blake could not dispute the evidence. Block number two. He did not know what to make of it. Did it matter now that all was said and done? Was there some greater significance? He had a feeling this was not his last time in contact with Satoshi Nakamoto. But for the moment, he enjoyed the cold beer and the barrage of warmly delivered insults from the three wild beasts he called his closest friends.

Blake reached over and rapped his knuckles on the bar.

For luck.

Because, well, it couldn't hurt.

CLICK HERE TO PRE-ORDER UNLEASHED, BLAKE BRIER BOOK TWO, NOW!

https://www.amazon.com/dp/B08J4DLX6D/

Printed in Great Britain
by Amazon

11602362R00129